Love
& LYRICS

JENNI B.

iUniverse

LOVE & LYRICS

iUniverse books may be ordered through booksellers or by contacting:

iUniverse
1663 Liberty Drive
Bloomington, IN 47403
www.iuniverse.com
844-349-9409

ISBN: 978-1-6632-5751-2 (sc)
ISBN: 978-1-6632-5750-5 (e)

Library of Congress Control Number: 2023920929

Print information available on the last page.

iUniverse rev. date: 10/26/2023

Chapter 1

In my humble opinion, this isn't my fault.

OK, fine. It's entirely my fault.

As I try to ignore the overly large, crisp envelope that keeps slapping against my thigh, I continue to jog down the street toward my car.

Stupid bulky letter.

If smaller, it could've fit in my backpack, but the university of Colorado insists on printing life-altering news on thick, elegant cardstock.

God, I could kill for a large espresso. Or a lethal injection of arsenic. Either would honestly do.

I sprint the last twenty feet to my car, throw open my driver's-side door, and slide in, where warmth is waiting for me.

My car is a mess—much like my life these days. It's filled with empty plastic coffee cups and takeout containers, and my gym bag is half open and spilling over in the backseat. But the state of my car is the least of my worries.

With a flick of my key, I turn over the ignition. The radio automatically turns on, blasting a song I spend half my days trying to get away from. I lean my head against my steering wheel and take some calming, deep breaths.

In. Out. In. Out.

I slowly look up to take in my surroundings while my car warms up, and I feel my heart drop to my stomach.

Two boys beam down at me from a skin-care billboard

advertisement. Their skin is clear, and their teeth are white and gleaming. The words under them read, "Shade uses Express Clear face wash on the road!"

I let out a sigh.

It's official: I've just hit rock bottom.

Outside on the sidewalk, I hear a couple of girls giggling and pointing up at the billboard. I inconspicuously roll down my window just enough to hear what they are giggling about. I might as well dig the salt into my aching heart more.

"He's so dreamy!" The tall blonde one sighs loudly. "Did you get tickets to the tour?"

"Obviously," her equally blonde friend says with an eyeroll.

"Do you think he'll sign my tablet?" The tall girl smirks. "That way, I can bring it to school. Lindsey will be so jealous!"

I narrowly resist the urge to snort. If only they knew that the cute Shade guitarist they are pining over used to think I was lying about the word *veggies* being short for *vegetables*. Or that he has a deathly fear of clowns.

It would be easy to ruin Aiden's life.

But I won't, obviously; I'm a good sister. Most of the time anyway.

After watching the pair of girls take selfies with the billboard behind them for a few moments, I roll my window up and pull my car away from the curb parking spot. The radio starts to play another Shade song, so I jab the power button off. I'd rather drive in silence than listen to Scott's voice. I let out a breathy sigh. It's unfair to punish the band and even Scott himself for my long-standing crush.

After Aiden and Scott were noticed in a local showcase, I quickly became a nobody compared to all the supermodels and sleek women who flocked to them. My blonde hair isn't radiant; at five foot five, I'm average height; and my pale skin makes it seem as if I would burn up in the sunlight like a vampire.

I continue driving, basking in the silence, casually passing the rows of manicured buildings and grand, luxurious houses that easily sell for a couple of cool million dollars. All kinds of folks wrapped in thick puffy coats hurry down the sidewalks through the cold, carrying bags labeled with *Gucci* or *Prada*. The cold has never bothered me. In fact, I used to take trips with Aiden and our dad up into the mountains to go snowboarding and skiing. But that was before. Now not so much. I stew in my thoughts as I pull into the underground parking of my parents' building. I punch the code from memory into the box, which lifts the gate, allowing me access.

As I step into the glass elevator of the apartment building, I feel a rising sense of panic.

This is OK. I'm OK. It's going to be OK, I repeat to myself like a mantra.

After all, Aiden was deported from Japan last year after the band accidentally set a sacred temple on fire. What harm could one little letter cause?

I stop outside my parents' apartment and wait a beat before I push the key in and open the door.

"Hello?"

Silence answers.

I blow out a breath. *Oh, thank God. They're still out shopping.*

My phone rings, shrill and loud, causing me to jump out of my skin. Then I see who is calling, and I let out a groan. Cautiously, I answer the FaceTime call.

"Hi, Ash."

"Well?" Ashley's impatient face fills my phone screen. "Have you told them about the letter yet?"

"They're not back yet."

"Typical." Ashley puckers her lips in disapproval, brushing her dark hair out of her eyes. "Let me guess. Aiden told them he'd pay for a shopping spree?"

"Apparently. Honestly, I can't keep track anymore."

I cross over to the fridge and take out ingredients, on autopilot. Miraculously, Dad has already eaten through most of the cheese and meat I dropped off last week, but there are still some carrots and mushrooms left. And wine. I purse my lips. *Vegetable stir fry maybe?*

"Seriously," Ashley says, "how much do you think Aiden spends on their apartment? Thousands? Millions?"

"Too much." I prop the phone up against the wall. "But it's not like Mom and Dad ask for it. Their careers—"

"Died in the eighties?" Ashley's voice is fond, despite her harsh words. "Never took off?"

"It's hard to be in the music industry, you know." I start chopping an onion into thin strips.

"Unless you're Aiden."

"Well, he got lucky."

Ashley snorts. "I'm sure he'd say it was raw talent."

I can't stop my smile. If it were anybody else, I would take offense, but Ashley knows Aiden almost as well as I do; Ashley's older brother, Scott, has been best friends with him for years.

Scott.

I dreamily push around the garlic and onion mixture in a hot skillet. *God, he's good looking.* I haven't seen him in ages, but even just thinking about his wild dark curls and green eyes is making me—

No. I jerk myself out of my forbidden thoughts. *Bad idea.*

He's Ashley's brother. She and I have a mutual understanding that our brothers are off-limits.

Yet I can't resist asking.

"How's Scott?" I ask casually. "After—" I feel my cheeks heating up, and I'm suddenly fascinated by the garlic I'm sautéing. "You know."

"After Scott was caught on camera half naked with a bunch of models in Europe, you mean?" Ashley grins knowingly.

"Ash!" I shriek, trying to cover the heat that's creeping up my neck.

"What?" She shrugs. "I called Scott to confirm. It's true. He partied a little harder than he intended for his twenty-fifth birthday." Her smile turns sly. "Why are you so interested?"

"I'm not."

"Liar."

I shove the garlic around with a spoon, trying to ignore the fact that my face feels as if it's on fire. I've never actually voiced my little crush on Scott to Ashley, but she would have to be walking around with a blindfold over her eyes not to notice it.

Thank God I'm able to deal with it now.

Growing up, I couldn't even get through dinner with Scott; I would sit at the kitchen table, all frizzy blonde hair, braces, and acne spots, and inevitably spill ketchup all over my top or burn my hand on a hot plate. I still cringe when I think about it.

"I'm just happy Aiden wasn't with Scott in Europe," I say, deftly changing the subject. "Or if Aiden was, he was smart enough not to get caught." I pause. "No offense."

"None taken." Ashley waves me off.

I watch as Ashley rubs her eyes and stuffs her feet into purple slippers. I glance at the clock, doing the mental gymnastics of calculating the time difference. It's past seven o'clock in Colorado, which means that in London, England, it's—

"Hang on." I frown. "Shouldn't you be asleep?"

"I'm still going out tonight."

I give her a dubious look. After our sophomore year in college, Ashley decided to study abroad. She's notorious for going out a lot, admittedly, but rarely in purple slippers.

"Aren't you going to change?"

"For the plane?" She grins. "Nah."

It takes a moment for my brain to understand, and when it does, I almost drop the knife into the stir fry. "You're flying back tonight?"

"Tomorrow, technically. It was supposed to be a surprise, but seeing as I leave for the airport in an hour—"

My phone rings, and I hold up a finger.

"Hold that thought," I tell her. "It's Soph." I can't keep the glee out of my voice. "She's going to grill you for not telling her that you're coming home, you know."

A few button pushes and a moment later, Sophia's face pops up on the screen. She's wearing a gloopy green face mask, and her shiny dark hair is swept into a top knot that, annoyingly, doesn't look ridiculous. I instantly hate her for it.

Even after five years of friendship, I can never quite forgive Sophia for constantly looking like a Vogue advertisement.

"I've just heard the news," Sophia says breathlessly.

My mind goes blank. I can feel the letter staring up at me from the counter, and for a split second, I think Sophia knows about it somehow.

But then Ashley groans and says, "You saw the tabloids then?"

"All of them," Sophia says gleefully. "Do you know there's a naked picture of Scott in the *Sunday Times*? I bought three copies."

Ashley pulls a face. "Gross, Soph."

"What?" she says, completely unabashed. "It's not my fault your brother has a body so fine that most of us would climb up him like a koala. What do you think, Carly?"

At the thought of a shirtless Scott, I feel my face turning the color of a stop sign again.

"Sure." I pour more white wine into the rice than is perhaps necessary. "Scott's body is fine."

"Fine?"

"Well, it's—"

"Fine?" Sophia repeats with a grin. "Anyway, you OK, Ash? I need to make sure before I spill the juiciest bit of gossip for you both."

"I'm OK," Ashley says, waving her off. "Mildly scarred from seeing my brother naked, but other than that, good. What's the gossip?"

Sophia brightens. "You all remember the old maple tree from high school? The one everyone called the Kissing Tree?"

I tune out slightly as Sophia launches into her monologue of gossip, choosing instead to focus on the stove and my rising anxiety. The Parmesan grater shakes in my hand. I glance nervously at the clock, half wishing for my parents to burst through the door so I can get this over with.

But alas.

"Carly?" Sophia asks gently.

I blink. It takes me a moment to realize they both are clearly waiting for me to respond to a question.

"Huh?" I say.

Ashley takes a sip of tea. "You know the school is chopping down the old Kissing Tree?"

"They're chopping it down?" I stop stirring. To my alarm, I can feel tears pricking at my eyes, and I immediately swipe at them. It's only a maple tree.

But it isn't.

It's the tree Ashley and I ate lunch together under for the first time, back when we were eleven and fresh at Cobblestone Academy. It's the tree I sat in while scribbling music lyrics on Sunday afternoons and the tree where I taught myself guitar. I even carved Scott's and my initials into the tree when I was twelve. Thankfully, neither Ashley nor Scott ever found them.

I love that tree.

"When?" I ask.

"Tomorrow," Sophia tells me gently. "Oh, Carly, I'm sorry. I thought you knew."

I set down the spoon. "It's fine." I manage a smile. "It's just a tree." Then I change the subject. "By the way, Ashley is coming home tomorrow."

Immediately, Sophia explodes into mayhem. "You're what?" she screams gleefully. "Oh my God!" She does a little dance. "We have to throw a party!"

"A party?" Ashley's eyes light up.

"With gingerbread martinis," Sophia says, seizing on the idea. "We can make it Christmas themed. I know someone who can cater."

"And mulled wine," I add dreamily. "So much mulled wine."

We are halfway through sorting out the details, when I hear keys jingle in the lock of the front door. I switch off the heat to the stir fry, and my mouth suddenly goes dry. I can tell that Ashley hears the noise too, because she looks at me solemnly, as if I'm a soldier departing for battle.

"That's my parents," I tell them. "I should go."

Ashley nods. "Good luck."

"Luck?" Sophia looks baffled. "Why does she need luck?"

"Fill her in," I tell Ashley glumly. "You have my permission."

I hang up the call.

A moment later, my mother sweeps into the room, stripping off her sodden hat and gloves. "Carly!" She kisses my cheek.

"What a surprise."

"It smells good, Carlz," my father says cheerfully, setting a collection of bright parcels on the side table. "Is that stir fry?"

Oh God.

He's looking at me so warmly that I want to sink into the floor and die. I'm going to have to tell them now, or I will undoubtedly chicken out. Slowly, I pick up the letter from the counter and extend it gingerly toward them as if it's a bomb that might explode.

"Here."

"Did you win an award, honey?" My mother frowns.

"Not really." I take a shaky breath. "Actually, I've failed out of college. I'm not going back."

"Excuse me?" My mom looks at me with eyes the size of saucers. "That is not an option."

"It's already happened, Mom." I push the envelope into her hands.

"You're seriously going to throw all your hard work out the window?" she shrieks, causing me to flinch.

"Well—"

"What about the plan for you to join my firm after graduation next semester? We have everything figured out!" my dad shouts as the situation sinks in.

"You had it figured out, Dad. Not me." I turn the stove off and grab my things. "This is a done deal. Let's continue this conversation after everyone calms down," I tell them gently before letting myself out of their apartment.

Chapter 2

"I'd like peonies for my funeral," I say gloomily. "Or roses. Either will work."

Ashley snorts. "It's December."

"So?"

"So, both of those are out of season." She plops a bottle of peppermint schnapps into the shopping basket I'm struggling to hold with the growing weight. "Oh, come on. Surely it wasn't that bad?"

"You have met my parents before, haven't you?"

Ashley rolls her eyes. "You mean the ones who practically raised Scott and me? Yeah, I have."

She starts placing a collection of colorful cans into the cart, stretching on her tiptoes to reach the top shelf. A sales assistant shoots her a suspicious look, and I don't blame him; with Ashley's short legs, brunette pigtails, and striped T-shirt, she can easily pass for fourteen.

"They want me to go back," I say to her, half-heartedly examining a bottle of red wine. "To repeat the year."

"But you don't want to?"

"I hate economics." I pull a face. "You know that."

"So, switch programs."

"To what?"

"Music. Obviously." She looks at me as if I've lost my mind.

"I can't."

"Because of Aiden?" She pinches the bridge of her nose. "Carly, you're so talented. Aiden shouldn't impact these kinds of decisions for you."

"It's not that simple, Ashley."

"Yes, it really is, Carly."

I grip the bottle of wine. Ashley makes it sound easy. But my parents are already angry at me for dropping out, so I can imagine how that conversation would go. As failed musicians themselves, my parents view studying music a lot like buying lottery tickets: often futile and meaningless and more likely to ruin your life than enhance it.

Then there's Aiden, the prodigy.

I set the bottle of wine back on the shelf, suddenly feeling exhausted. Shade is a chart-topping world-class band. They've won a few Grammy awards, including the Album of the Year award, and countless others I can never remember.

I can never live up to him.

I blow out a breath. No, music is out of the question. Studying economics at Colorado State is now out of the question.

"What else are you going to do?" Ashley makes a face as she examines a packet of shimmery crystals that dissolve in champagne. "Live on your parents' couch?"

"Absolutely not."

"Well, there would be worse places to live." She chuckles.

"Look!" I seize a gaudy plastic Santa Claus, mostly to distract her, and waggle my eyebrows. "What do you think?"

"There's no way that's making its way into Sophia's house."

"Really?"

"Go on then." She crosses her arms, smirking. "I dare you."

For a moment, I consider it; then I picture Sophia's sleek, modern house, with its white shag rugs and rose-gold bar cart, and I swiftly set the ugly Santa down.

"It wouldn't make it past the front door."

Ashley hands over her ID at the checkout, and the elderly woman takes her time in examining it, holding it up to the light and checking for any reason to doubt the legitimacy of it. I duck out of sight to hide a smile. Ashley turned twenty-two last month, but sales assistants never believe her. It drives her nuts.

Sure enough, Ashley looks thunderstruck as a manager is called over.

"Unbelievable," she mutters as soon as we exit the store with arms laden with plastic shopping bags. "You wouldn't believe the things I go through as a short person."

Once we have everything loaded into the trunk of Ashley's Jeep, we make our way back to my place. My apartment isn't anything close to the level of sophistication of my parents'. But it's still charming and has everything I need. Ashley smoothly parks in one of the empty spaces across from the door of my building. Together we load our arms with sacks and head inside.

Some of my friends give me grief for not using the money Aiden graciously gives us all on a nicer place, a fancy car, or really anything. They don't understand that I've never once asked for a penny from my brother. Oh, he offers, but I always say no. I do just fine with my part-time job and the money my parents gave me when I graduated from high school. They set up savings accounts for both my brother and me to go to college. Only Aiden didn't go to college and probably never will now. So, he dumped his account into mine, doubling what I would have received otherwise. I didn't know about that until a few months after I received the money. When I broached the subject with Aiden, he shrugged it off and told me the money would be better spent with me than him. That and he was making plenty with Shade on tour. I dropped it after that.

We reach the top of the second flight of stairs, and I struggle to get my key into the lock. With a flick of my wrist, the lock clicks, and I push the door open with my shoulder. I flip on the lights inside the door, and we make our way to my kitchen and living room area. I don't spend much time here, so everything is sparse and mostly clean. I spend most of my time at school or at work. I suppose without school now, I'll probably be around here more often. I mull that around in my head for a moment.

The cream-colored walls, the light brown hardwood floors, and the stark white ceilings give the rooms a warm and welcoming feel, taking the notice away from how small the overall apartment is. The two floor-to-ceiling windows on the far wall of the living room are separated by my personal favorite feature: the stone gas fireplace.

My sectional couch fills up half the living room and is perfect for getting cozy with a good book and a glass of wine. Against the side wall, pushed into a corner, a pair of large bookcases are crammed with an assortment of papers, books, and board games. Against the other wall is a small white wooden desk. I've paired an ergonomic black chair that allows me to get work done or get lost in writing music for hours. Stuffed under the desk is a woven wastepaper basket overflowing with crumpled paper and debris. The wall above the desk is completely taken up by my corkboard.

My kitchen is set up for someone with great cooking abilities. I've always had a gift when it comes to cooking and baking. It's well-known to everyone in my life that I'm the go-to girl when it comes to whipping up a dessert or a meal. The thought of opening a side business for it has crossed my mind a few times, but I just don't think it's my calling.

Ashley shuffles into the kitchen and places the shopping bags on the counter, looking at my empty white walls. She purses her lips but doesn't comment on them.

"We should start to get ready," I tell her as I turn and head down the short hallway to my bedroom.

Without pausing, I open my door and flip the lights on. As we walk into my bedroom, we are stopped short by my bed, which takes up most of the room. I've hung silver-colored drapes that fall elegantly down the floor-to-ceiling windows. I walk inside my overly large walk-in closet with Ashley on my heels.

"You could wear your red jumper," Ashley says as she reaches for one of my black dresses.

"Well, it's not very festive," I say, mostly because I know Ashley will try to convince me to wear it otherwise. "What about my red top?"

"It's versatile," she says defensively, and I roll my eyes.

"Fine. I'll wear the jumper," I say with a half smile.

"OK." Ashley grabs her phone. "I'm calling Sophia to get her butt over here."

By the time Sophia arrives, Ashley and I are halfway through a bottle of white wine. At the sound of a knock at the door, Ashley, giddy with excitement and chardonnay, springs gleefully from the bed and tackles her like a linebacker.

"My hair!" Sophia squeals. "Ash, you'll ruin it!" She tries unsuccessfully to bat Ashley off, but Ashley only clings tighter, like a barnacle to a rock. "Oh, for God's sake."

"You missed me," Ashley says in a singsong voice. "Admit it."

"I didn't."

"You did." Ashley pokes her cheek. "I can tell."

Sophia sighs. Her blonde hair is elegantly swept into an elaborate updo, and she's already wearing heels, eyeliner, and a perfume that smells like roses and vanilla. Her fingernails are painted nude.

"Oh, come on. You both need to get changed. Now." Sophia ushers us off the bed. "We need to get going. I need to get to the party for the caterers, and someone needs to do damage control for any issues."

We both change quickly. Ashley wiggles into a green halter dress the same shade as her eyes, and I put on my red satin jumper, which doesn't completely wash out my light features. Admittedly, the neckline is deeper than I'm comfortable with, but it will do.

It's a short ride to Sophia's house in the Village. I can tell by the booming bass from a DJ that the party is picking up, and we are only two steps through the door, when someone presses a gingerbread martini into my hand. I twist my neck to see who and only catch the back of a server.

"We made it," Ashley announces, as if she might not have shown up to her own coming-to-town party.

We exchange pleasantries with some of the elites Sophia has invited. Halfway through a conversation, I sneakily press the martini into Ashley's hand. She takes it without question and takes a large swallow. This is our silent system: Ashley takes the drinks, and I take care of her later.

A handsome guy whose name we don't know is halfway through a story about a basketball game, when Ashley's eyes darken.

"Oh shit," she mutters.

"What?"

Ashley tips her head subtly. "Look."

I follow her gaze and then groan. "Quick," I say, grabbing her hand. "She hasn't seen us. There's still time."

But alas, there isn't time.

"Ashley!" A leggy blonde with caked-on makeup materializes next to us. "Oh my God. I saw the papers; you must be so devastated." She touches Ashley's arm. "How's Scott holding up?"

Ashley shoots daggers at the blonde's hand as if wishing she could impale it with her high heel, and I manage to cover a smile. Unfortunately, my smile is wiped away when I realize the random guy has managed to slip away, leaving us alone with Alex.

The traitor.

"He's fine," Ashley says shortly.

"The poor thing," Alex replies. "He must just want to forget about it."

"I'm sure he does."

"If only people would stop talking about it," Alex says with such sincerity that I cough to hide a laugh. Unfortunately, the noise alerts Alex to my presence. "And how's Aiden? Is he back in town anytime soon?" she asks with a slight bit of venom in her voice.

"No, no." I wave her off. "Not for months. They're just about to start the next tour."

As if Alex doesn't already know.

"Well, I'm having a little get-together next week," Alex says a little too casually. "So, if Aiden's in town, let him know he's welcome to stop by. Scott too."

"And us?" Ashley asks sweetly. "Are we welcome to stop by?"

For a moment, Alex looks baffled. "Oh, of course." She takes a sip of champagne. "I thought that was implied," she says with a wink.

Ashley drains the rest of the gingerbread martini and wipes foam off the top of her lip. "You'll have to excuse us," she says, linking her arm through mine. "Our drinks need refilling."

I lean closer as we make our way toward the drinks table, which is piled high with golden glasses, bottles of champagne, and platters of party treats. "We're not really going to her party, right?"

"Oh, hell no!" Ashley snorts. "Over my dead body."

"It was bad enough when the guys were here and she was attached to them like a leech, but we still can't seem to shake her." I groan.

"Let's put her out of our minds."

The party, thankfully, starts to improve. I catch sight of Sophia gliding around the room; her tinkling laugh echoes off the large glass windows as she flits from group to group. Ashley, to nobody's surprise, ends up dancing on a table.

That leaves me, inevitably, in the kitchen.

I've developed a routine during these parties: wash the dishes, mop the floors, and sort out the garbage. Mercifully, there are fewer dishes tonight. Usually, I'm the one who makes food beforehand, but Sophia's catering company has saved me hours of work.

Just as I'm reaching for the mop, my phone rings. My brother's obnoxious face fills the screen. I smile as I swipe across the screen to answer.

"Hey, weirdo."

"Well, well," Aiden drawls. "If it isn't the university dropout."

"Oh, shut it." I roll my eyes.

"Mom and Dad just told me the news." He sounds amused.

"Should I be worried, impressed, or grateful you took the spotlight off Scott's photos for me?" He chuckles.

"You should be celebrating," I say gloomily. "You're going to inherit everything now. Mom's going to write me out of the will."

"She'll calm down." Aiden pauses. "You know, eventually."

I exit the kitchen, slipping out onto the balcony. "What makes you so sure?"

"I stole the car, got a speeding ticket, and gambled the clothes off my back all in one weekend, remember?" Aiden must be plucking a guitar, because I can hear music. "And she's not angry with me anymore."

"You bought her a brand-new Porsche," I say. "My regular student budget can't accommodate things like that."

"You're not a student."

"Ouch."

"Too soon?" He strums a chord. "I was testing the waters."

I lean against the cold railing. The frigid December air nips at my bare thighs, causing me to involuntarily shiver. I bounce up and down on my toes for warmth. I can see the Colorado skyline glittering below like a sea of shimmering stars in the black night.

"I can't go back there, Aid."

"I know." His voice softens. "You shouldn't have to."

"But what am I going to do?" I feel panic rising inside me; the half bottle of wine is fueling the flames of it in my chest. "I have no skills except for a freakish knowledge of Bach."

"You're a rockstar in the kitchen," he says with a chuckle.

"I know you don't mean that in a sexist way." I can't help but grin.

"Why don't you just fly by the seat of your pants for a bit? See where life takes you for once?"

I grip the railing. *No, not an option.*

"Maybe I should work at a coffee shop," I say blandly. "I like coffee."

"Too dull."

"What about a secretary?" I let out a sigh. "I hear there are lots of sexy CEOs around hiring."

I can practically hear Aiden's scowl as he says, "Not funny, Carlz. And completely out of the question. Do you know what some of those powerful CEOs are capable of?"

"That," I say, "is incredibly sexist."

"You're right." Aiden sounds exhausted. "Sorry. But I'm not wrong on that. Besides, I have a better idea of how you can fill your time."

"Go snowboarding? Become a professional beer pong player?"

"No," Aiden says with a hint of irritation. "Why don't you come on tour with me?"

"You can't be serious," I stutter after a moment of silence.

"Dead serious. Just promise me you won't try to steal any shows or anything," he says with a chuckle.

"Aiden!" I gasp in horror. "You know I would never."

"Hey, I've got to say it. I've seen some crazy things on tour. I feel like anything is possible," he says a little dejectedly.

"Besides, Aiden, music is your thing. It always has been. Right?" I ask him nervously.

"Right," he says simply. "I've got the music; you've got the brains."

"Exactly."

We end our call, and I can't help but think things just got worse in a way.

⋘◆⋙

"I can't go," I say. "You don't think I should. Right?"

I pass a mug of steaming hot chocolate to Ashley, who is currently sitting next to the toilet in her en suite, occasionally hurling her guts out like a drowning sailor while clutching the toilet seat like a life preserver. I gently stroke her hair. Next to us, Sophia, wearing a fluffy white bathrobe, is painting her nails devil red.

"I think you should go," Sophia says for the millionth time. "When else will you get the chance to tour with the most famous band in the world?"

"I wasn't aware the Beatles were still touring." I feign surprise.

"Funny."

"I think so."

Sophia points her nail polish brush at me sternly. "If you don't go, you're insane."

"What's insane," Ashley says, looking slightly green still, "is that there are two of you right now." She shields one eye with a hand, squinting up at me.

"Look, I can't just go on tour." I bounce up and start pacing. "It's—"

"Stop!" Ashley yelps, cringing. "Just stand still or sit back down!"

"Sorry."

"I wish I hadn't had so many drinks," Ashley growls, clutching the pillow on the floor next to her tighter. "I feel as if an army of jackhammers has taken up residence in my head."

"Poor baby," I croon, stroking her hair some more.

21

"Those martinis were lethal." She smiles at me. "I agree with Soph; you should go, Carlz. Break the rules for once."

I stare at her. She once cried when she forgot to return an overdue library book, so the fact that she's telling me to break the rules is nothing short of miraculous.

"But I won't know anyone," I say, chewing my lip. "And the boys will be rehearsing most days. What if I get lonely?"

"Well, I'll go with you," Ashley says casually, as if she's suggesting we grab an ice cream cone. "My classes don't start for a few more months, and I haven't seen Scott in ages." She sits up, looking less green. "We could both join for the first few weeks of the tour."

"You mean it?"

"Sure. Why not?"

"Oh, you're kidding me!" Sophia throws her hands up. "So, you're both going to jet around the United States while I rot in Colorado?" She jabs a finger in my direction. "Where's the justice in that?"

"You have a photo shoot with *Cosmo* next week, Soph. I don't think you'll exactly be suffering." I roll my eyes.

"True." Sophia holds up a hand, admiring her handiwork. "And you can bring me back that face cream I like from New York."

"There are face creams in Colorado, you know," I say, and Sophia smiles sheepishly.

"I know." She grins.

I steal Ashley's hot chocolate and take a sip of the warmth to steady myself.

This is a bad idea. In fact, it's a bad idea of epic proportions. I just failed out of university; I don't deserve to travel the country. I deserve to spend my days grinding espresso beans at Starbucks and getting shouted at by middle-aged mothers for mixing up a latte and a cappuccino. I can't just run away from my problems.

And yet …

I pass the hot chocolate back to Ashley, pursing my lips. Up until now, I've tried to be the perfect daughter. I got a scholarship in economics because my father wanted me to. I got into the best business school in Colorado because my mother asked me to. I've tried to be the perfect sister. I don't share any personal information online about Aiden or our lives because he's asked me not to.

Don't I deserve to do something I want to do? Don't I deserve to spend some time with my brother? Don't I deserve to have some fun for once?

A small voice inside me whispers, "Plus, Scott will be around."

I shove the small voice away, giving myself a mental head slap. "Let's say I do go," I say slowly. "How would we get there? It's the December holidays; airlines are booked solid."

"We'll fly private," Ashley says. "The boys will send a plane."

"And what about money? I don't want Aiden to—"

"If you say, 'bankroll my lifestyle' right now, I'll kill you."

I frown. Up until now, I have refused to take a penny from Aiden. He's offered to pay for my education, a new car, and anything he thinks will make my life a million times easier. I would rather be up to my ears in debt and work full-time at a music store than take money from him.

Ashley has fewer qualms.

Besides, Ashley's family owns a sizable estate in Northern California and a holiday home in upstate New York. I don't think she has ever had to think all that much about money.

"Oh, come on." Sophia sighs. "Don't make us post that video of you falling asleep face down in a bowl of spaghetti after a night of clubbing on Facebook."

"Is that a threat?" I ask them, taken aback.

"It's an incentive."

"What if I still refuse to go?"

Sophia's smile turns wicked. "Oh, trust me: after we post that video, you'll be begging to leave the country."

"But how will I explain this to my parents?" I stutter.

"Carly, you need to stop worrying about them. This is about you," Ashley says.

That is how, two hours later, I find myself packing a suitcase and going through my flight itinerary.

It doesn't take me long to clean up my apartment and let my building manager know I'll be gone for a while. I finish loading my bags into the trunk of my car and get in before I start to freeze to death. My phone buzzes a few times in my cup holder, signaling a text message has come through. I glance at the text.

It's from Aiden: "The plane will be waiting for you. Let security know who you are, and show them ID. They'll take care of you and Ashley. I know you stole my Denver hockey jersey—bring it with you."

I smile to myself. *Typical Aiden. Simple and to the point.*

Then I remember what I'm about to do, and my smile falters.

I put my car in Drive and head to my parents' place—in other words, hell.

Part of me hopes my parents are out again, but my dad opens the door almost immediately after I knock. He's dressed in a gray sweater and jeans, and there's a mug of coffee in his hand. His eyes are red-rimmed.

My heart twists and drops to my stomach; I know it's because of me.

"Hi!" He gently pulls me in for a hug. "Come in."

He ushers me into the living room, where my mom sets down a stack of sheet music. My throat feels dry as sand. I've deliberately left my luggage in my car—no need to tip them off early—but I still feel as if they can read the guilt on my face.

"I've got something to tell you," I blurt out.

In retrospect, I realize it was not, perhaps, the best opening line.

My mom turns white. "Oh my God. You're pregnant, aren't you?"

"What? No!" I stutter.

But my mom is undeterred. "That's why you failed out of school, isn't it?" She takes my hands. "Don't worry, honey. We'll support you. Even if the father is that rude Adam boy you used to see, we'll—"

"Mom!" I shake loose of her grip. "I'm not pregnant!"

"Oh." Her face tightens. "Is it Aiden? Did something happen to him?"

"Aiden's fine." I collapse onto the couch. "The only problem he has these days is deciding which backup dancer to date this week."

Unfortunately, my mother seizes on this. "He's dating someone?" she says.

"It was illustrative." I resist the urge to roll my eyes. "You know Aiden doesn't date. He's paranoid about having his secrets leaked to the press."

"Poor Aiden." My dad sighs.

It doesn't matter that Aiden is one of the most successful musicians in North America, is swimming in money, and can get any girl he wants; our father will continue to pity him for having to deal with, and I quote, "the pitfalls of fame."

Aiden can buy a Tesla in cash, and our father still feels bad for him.

"Well, this is kind of about Aiden," I say, backtracking. "At least a little bit."

"Oh?"

I take a deep breath. "I'm going on tour with him. I'm leaving today."

There's a long, drawn-out pause.

"You're joking," my dad croaks out.

"You think running from this mess is the best way to handle this?" Mom jumps to her feet and starts shouting. "We raised you better than this!"

I've prepared myself for these hysterics. I brace myself through the shouting, letting my parents get it all out. My dad bangs a fist on the coffee table.

"Carly, what is with you? Your mother's right. We raised you so much better than this! You need to stay here and figure out your next steps!" he shouts at me.

"Excuse me?" I blink.

"Are you going deaf?" my mom shouts. "This is the last thing you should be doing!"

"Mom, Dad," I say slowly, "you know I'm not going back to college, right? I need to do this for me. Aiden is giving me this as a break, not to run away." I try to stay calm.

"Fine. We will talk once you're back." My mom turns her back to me and disappears down the hallway, slamming a door closed.

And that's that.

I look over at my dad, expecting him to continue yelling. Instead, he follows my mom down the hall and disappears. I take that as my cue to leave. I let myself out and make my way to my car.

Once I'm in my car, I take a few shaky breaths to calm myself down. *That wasn't much different from how I pictured it going.* The ringing of my phone breaks the silence in my car.

"Ashley." I sigh, not bothering to check the caller ID. "I'm on my way." I shove my key into the ignition and turn my car over. "You are not going to believe what I just went through. Not only did my mom think I was pregnant, but apparently, I'm ruining my life."

"Well, are you?" The husky voice of Scott floats through my phone.

I slam on my brakes, jerk to a stop, and drop my phone. My heart seems to be in my stomach, and my stomach seems to be at my feet.

"Scott." I breathe out as I fumble with my phone and my heart rate. "I wasn't expecting ... I thought—"

"Calm down, Carlz." His voice is gentle and soothing. "Are you OK?"

"You know that nickname makes me feel like I'm seven."

"I know," Scott says easily. "That's why I use it," he adds teasingly.

I frown. I can hear music blaring in the background, or maybe it's a video game. It wouldn't be out of this realm for him to be at a party either. But I can also picture him at home alone, eating a bag of chips or a bowl of popcorn in his gray sweatpants.

I like Scott best that way. Sober. Teasing. Mildly irritating. Effortlessly sexy.

"So," he says, "I hear you're flying out here shortly."

"Yeah." I pause to pull out onto the highway. "I'm heading to pick Ashley up now."

I'm met with silence. I know why he's really calling.

"Look, Scott—"

"It's none of my business." He cuts me off firmly. "And it's not anybody else's either."

"I know." I breathe out.

"Carly?"

"Yeah?"

"Are you OK?"

It's a simple question. But I feel tears prick at my eyes. Scott is one of the few who has ever witnessed firsthand how hard my parents are on me. He and Ashley were over all the time while we were growing up.

"I will be." I try to keep my tears out of my voice. "I wish I could go back just to please them, but I can't. Not this time."

"I know."

My heart flutters a little bit. His simple understanding is like a balm to my anxiety. I turn down the street toward Ashley's place as I say, "Economics isn't for me. To be honest, the stress of putting myself through those classes was starting to make me physically sick."

"Yeah, Aiden told me that too."

His flat tone confuses me, and I frown at my phone.

"I'm sorry I haven't called you lately," I tell him as I park. I know I sound exhausted.

"It's a two-way street, Carlz. I'm sorry too," he says in an equally exhausted voice.

Even exhausted, his voice still sends goose bumps across my

arms and sends my heart racing. Not that I can ever admit that out loud to him or anyone. First, telling him I've been in love with him for most of my life could mean absolute rejection from him. Second, Aiden can never find out. He has never handled my having boyfriends well. This would be like dropping a bomb on him.

"Well, I'm excited to see you. It's been too long," he says.

"It has been a long time." My heart flutters a bit more. I bite my lip. "You won't tell Aiden about my parents' pregnancy accusation, will you? I'm really not sleeping with anyone." I pause. "At least not recently."

"I gotchu, girl," Scott says cheerfully. "Bye, Carlz."

He ends the call before I get a chance to say goodbye.

Chapter 3

I spend most of the plane ride bouncing off the walls with anxiety and fascination. Despite having an ultrafamous brother, I hardly ever travel, and I've never been on the band's private jet. I'm fascinated by everything inside the jet. I make a fuss over the sleek leather seats and then over all the tiny soaps in the small bathroom. I'm just praising the secret stash of Belgian chocolate bars, when the pilot announces that we are beginning our descent into Los Angeles.

"Oh, good," Ashley says, sounding relieved. "We're here."

I crane my neck, looking out the window. Los Angeles is a patchwork of glittering glass towers and long sweeps of beaches curling around the blue water. The sight of palm trees instead of mountains makes my heart soar.

"It's so pretty," I murmur.

"How badly do you want to party on the beach tonight?" Ashley cracks a smile.

"You think the guys will let us?" I ask her with a devious smile.

"I don't think we need their permission." She chuckles. "But since they are our brothers, we should probably let them know. Out of courtesy." She giggles.

"You know what, Ash?" I shake my head. "I'm happy we're doing this."

Once we disembark the plane, I manage to pick out four people waiting for us: Aiden, Scott, their bandmate Cole, and their long-suffering manager, Julie. My eyes meet Scott's, and I feel my heart do a backflip and turn itself inside out.

No. I chastise myself. *Bad. Stop it.*

"Carly!"

A moment later, Aiden sprints across the tarmac, lifts me up into a crushing hug, and spins me in a circle. He turns and starts on Ashley next, squeezing her so hard that he knocks her sunglasses off.

"Aiden!" Ashley squeals, batting at his shoulder. "Those are expensive!"

"I'll buy you new ones." He grins at her.

"Yeah, OK." Ashley scoffs.

Cole reaches us next. I haven't seen him since the guys did a show in Colorado more than a year ago, and he has somehow become even more handsome in person. His broad shoulders have filled out, and his acne has cleared up, leaving his dark skin smooth. Plus, he has finally ditched the terrible gold glasses he once thought were trendy. He grew up with the boys and seemed to melt into the band naturally.

"Well, well." Cole grins at Ashley. "Here comes trouble."

"Oh, shut up, Cole." Ashley smacks his shoulder, but she looks pleased. "You've gotten taller."

"And you've gotten shorter," Cole says.

"Don't start with me."

"Wouldn't dream of it." Cole holds up his hands. "Hey, Carly." He then adds cheekily, "You're looking tall. Did you grow?"

"You have a death wish, Cole Johnson." I grin up at him.

Then Scott reaches us, and I forget how to breathe.

He's dressed in a plain white T-shirt under a black leather jacket. His dark jeans are a contrast to the board shorts the other guys are wearing. I drink in the sight of him as he approaches: his dark brown hair, his green eyes, and the small white scar under his chin from a fistfight years ago. Only the slight purplish circles under his eyes seem to be different—a sign of exhaustion.

My stupid staccato heart skips three beats.

"Hi, Carlz." Scott kisses my cheek. "How was the flight?"

"The best." By some miracle, I manage not to hyperventilate, and I produce a normal smile. "Do you know private jets have chocolate bars?"

"I'm sure you sampled one." He grins down at me.

"Three—or four, if you count the one, I stole for later," I say.

"That's my girl." He wraps an arm across my shoulders and then ruffles my hair as if I'm twelve years old again.

I want to melt into the pavement and die.

Next to me, Ashley frowns. "Hey, what am I? A groupie?"

"Family can't be groupies?" Scott looks amused.

Nevertheless, he gives his sister a small peck on the cheek. Then, without further ado, he bends down and scoops up both of our bags. Julie almost drops her clipboard.

"What are you doing?" she hisses. "Scott, if you pull a muscle before the show tomorrow, I swear to God I will quit."

"Relax, Jules," Scott drawls. "I've got it."

Julie doesn't look convinced. She's clutching the clipboard so hard her knuckles are turning white, and she looks on the verge of a breakdown. Then again, I reflect, Aiden once said Julie spends most of her days on the verge of a breakdown; she's just better at hiding it most days. I frequently forget that Julie is only twenty-nine. These boys probably have her sprouting gray hairs already.

"Right." Julie sighs. "Shall we go then?"

As we make our way toward the waiting limos, I fall into step with Ashley and Aiden.

"Where's Kyle?" Ashley asks.

"Still at the hotel." Aiden frowns. "Why?"

"Oh, no reason," Ashley says airily. "I'm just excited to meet him—that's all."

"Really?" Aiden gives her a hard look.

"He is your fourth bandmate, isn't he now?"

"I see," Aiden says slowly. "So it has nothing to do with the fact that *People* magazine just ranked Kyle the Sexiest Man Alive?"

"Did they?" Ashley says with a mischievous grin. "I had no idea."

I turn my laugh into a hacking cough. I know for a fact Ashley currently has a copy of the magazine lying on the coffee table in her apartment. I've seen it in the background of our video calls. But I choose not to give her away.

"I'm excited to meet him too," I say, trying to lighten the mood. "He's from Australia, right?"

Aiden nods. "Thank God Scott convinced him to join. When Nate dropped out last year, I thought Shade was going to be toast."

I study his face for any animosity, but Aiden seems genuinely relaxed, and I breathe a sigh of relief. When Nate dropped out of the band last year to pursue college, I thought the boys would never forgive him. But now Nate is crushing exams, and Kyle is killing it on the drums.

Everyone is happy.

It doesn't take long to reach the hotel; even with the insane Los Angeles traffic, it takes only an hour or so. I'm dying to use the bathroom by the time we arrive. The hotel is right on the beach, so the sounds of the waves and the trickling of the dolphin fountains don't help matters.

"Can you text me the room number?" I grip Ashley's arm.

"Where are you off to? Are you OK?"

"Bathroom."

"Oh! OK." Ashley sighs theatrically, as if I'm causing her a great inconvenience. "Please hurry! We need to pick out our outfits before dinner."

With that, I'm off like a racehorse.

After a frantic exchange with a startled bellboy, I sprint toward the nearest bathroom, trying to ignore the feeling that my bladder is about to burst. I'm just rounding the corner, when I collide with something solid and heavy.

"Shit!" a voice says, and the accent isn't lost on me. "Bloody hell."

I stop in my tracks. There's a boy kneeling in front of me. His hands scramble to pick up his fallen keys and phone. Although I can only see the top of his blond head, I know who it is: Kyle, Aiden's fourth bandmate.

I clear my throat. "Are you—"

"Kyle Hansen?" He interrupts me with a sigh. "Yes, I am."

"I was going to say *all right*, actually."

"Oh." His face flushes with color. "Right."

He rises to his feet. Standing this close, I can smell the warm and spicy cologne clinging to his skin. There's a dimple to the left of his mouth, and I feel a bizarre urge to reach out and touch it. I can see why *People* named him the Sexiest Man Alive.

"So"—Kyle shuffles awkwardly—"do you want a photograph or something?"

Too late, I realize that Kyle thinks I'm a fan.

"Oh no," I blurt out. "No, that's OK. I was just on my way to—" I gesture vaguely down the hallway. "You know, freshen up."

Immediately, I want to kick myself.

"I should go," I say simply.

I sprint the rest of the way toward the bathroom, only stopping once I'm safely through the doors. Like a coward, I take my time, slathering on complimentary vanilla lotion and combing my hair with my fingers, until Ashley texts me with the room number. I'm still riding on an adrenaline high as I take the elevator up to the top floor, the penthouse suites. Thankfully, I don't run into any of the guys.

When I enter our room, Ashley is kneeling on top of a mountain of clothes.

"What do you think?" she asks, holding up something sparkly and silver for my inspection. "Is this too much?"

"Depends on where we're going." I shrug.

"The Reserve."

The way she says the name makes it clear I'm supposed to know where that is.

"I see." I kneel next to her. "So the dress code is short and sparkly?"

"You have no idea what I'm talking about, do you?" She looks at me with an exasperated expression.

"Not a clue."

"Pull the place up on your phone while I do your hair." She lets out a sigh.

An hour later, we are ready to head out. The boys have a sound check, so we pile into the waiting limo alone. They intend to meet up with us later in the evening. I sit back and start to relax while sipping the free champagne as Los Angeles whips by outside. Ashley rolls down a window, and we breathe in the warm, humid air.

"So," Ashley says in her serious voice, "Cole."

"What about him?"

"I'm in love with him."

"What?" I choke on my champagne.

"OK, not actually," Ashley says, rolling her eyes. "But you have to admit he's a smoke show now." She adjusts the strap of one of her heels. "Do you think Scott or Aiden would care if I slept with him?"

"Yes," I say firmly. "They'd kill him."

"Such a shame."

"What about Kyle?" My voice comes out as a squeak, and I pray Ashley doesn't notice. "I thought you were interested in him."

"I like looking at his face," Ashley says. "We'll see about his personality."

The limo drops us off at the top of an enormous cliff. A glass restaurant is positioned just a few feet from the edge, like a glittering tear about to fall off the edge of an eyelash, and as we draw closer, I realize the sea below is lit up with an eerie blue light. I can just barely make out bright yellow fish and slippery moss-green eels swimming below.

I'm practically overwhelmed by the club scene in front of me: colored strobe lights; speakers; a stage; bars with barstools; small, round tables with stools; waitresses dressed skimpily, with glowing trays of drinks, shooters, or empty bottles and glasses; shots lined up at the bar; and sophisticated-looking bartenders.

It's the coolest thing I've ever seen.

I can feel people staring as the waiter leads us to a table on a glass floor, and I tug at my dress, self-consciously pulling it farther down my thighs. Sophia managed to convince me to buy it last year, but I never intended to wear it, until now.

Now I remember why.

"Ashley," I hiss in her direction, "people are staring."

"Of course they are."

"But why?"

"Because we're hot, obviously." She looks at me in exasperation.

The waiter comes over, and Ashley orders a bottle of champagne and a few appetizers. We both produce our IDs, and he takes them with a smile. I see recognition flash in his eyes as he takes note of our last names.

"I'll be your waiter all evening. Please don't hesitate to flag me down," he says as he hands us back our IDs.

"Perfect." Ashley bats her eyelashes flirtatiously up at him.

As soon as the waiter disappears, I let out a breath.

"You're going to scare the poor guy." I chuckle.

"Me? Nah, never."

I reach for a bread roll and shred it as we wait for the waiter to return with the champagne. I shift my weight between my heels as I take in the entirety of our view of the ocean.

I'm just about to launch into a speech about responsibility and giving the wrong perception, when the door we came through moments ago opens, and Scott enters.

All coherent thoughts blow out of my ears.

Oh my, that man looks damn good in a suit.

I'm still staring as Scott draws closer, and it takes me a moment to realize he is staring at me too. His eyes climb the length of my bare thighs.

"Carly," he chokes out. "What on earth are you wearing?"

"It's a dress," Ashley snaps, jumping to my defense. "Perhaps you've heard of them before?"

"That dress is way too short." His eyes turn a darker shade of green as they meet mine.

"I second that," Aiden says as he, Cole, and Kyle materialize next to Scott.

"By at least six inches," Scott adds.

I'm not sure what comes over me exactly, but the next words out of my mouth are certainly not planned.

"I'm surprised you can measure six inches," I say coolly, "seeing as you've never seen anything that long before."

There's a long, drawn-out pause. Then Kyle begins to cackle.

"Oh shit." Cole coughs. "Little Carlz has claws." Then he reaches behind him.

I brace myself as I take in the young man now tucked under Cole's arm.

"Ashley, this is Kyle. He's our new drummer."

I cringe inwardly as Ashley extends a hand to Kyle.

Cole turns toward me. "And this is—"

"You," Kyle says, looking caught off guard. "I know you."

"You do?" Scott arches an eyebrow, and his tone is blank.

"You do?" Ashley repeats, turning to face me.

"Not really," I say. "We bumped into each other earlier today." I can feel heat rushing up my neck.

"You met Kyle at the hotel?" Ashley says, raising her eyebrows until they reach her hairline. "And you didn't think to tell me?"

"Well, I didn't really meet him," I stutter desperately. "I ran into him."

"Literally." Kyle smirks.

"Sorry about that. You don't have any lasting injuries, do you?"

"Just my pride."

"I'm sure Kyle's fine," Scott says. His voice is sharp like a knife. "Can we sit down, get some drinks, get some food, and just chill, please?"

Without saying anything, we all take seats, and Scott drops into the chair beside me.

"If you don't mind me asking, what do you do outside of this tour, Carly?" Kyle asks as we sit down.

"Well, I—"

"She's got the brains out of the two of us." Aiden interrupts me. "I've got the music, and she's got the brains. Right, Carly?" He grins.

"Right." I choke out an agreement. I feel guilt rise up inside me.

"Oh, so you're in college?" Kyle asks, seemingly interested.

"Well, I—"

"Not anymore. She's taking a gap year." Aiden again answers for me.

"Whoa. Aiden, I never said anything about a gap year. In fact, I never said anything about going back to school at all," I tell him sternly. The air around our table gets more awkward.

"Well, what else are you going to do?" Aiden shrugs nonchalantly.

"How about you stay out of my business?" The blood starting to pound in my ears is a pretty good indicator I'm about to lose my temper on my brother in the middle of this club.

"Hey now. Both of you chill. We can hash this stuff out at a different location and a different time," Ashley says coldly and sternly, mostly toward Aiden.

Aiden just shrugs. I make a mental note of Aiden's strange behavior.

It takes a bit before we all seem to fall into a rhythm and start to relax into the music and environment. It's not until later that I notice Scott hasn't said much to either Kyle or me since he arrived, which is out of character for him. I subconsciously pull at the hem of my skirt as I ponder what's going on with him.

Chapter 4

I haven't always been in love with Scott. When we were all young, he was just my older brother's best friend. Back then, Scott was often around my house, eating hot dogs, hiding bugs in my room, and annoying me in any way he could dream up.

Of course, Scott was never entirely carefree.

I hate this part of Scott and Ashley's story. I try not to think about it often, because it makes my heart ache for them. When they were young, their older sister went on a hike in the mountains with friends, and she didn't come back.

I don't know the details. Ashley never speaks about it. But I know their parents both threw themselves into their respective jobs—so much so that they shipped Scott and Ashley off to Cobblestone Academy.

That was where Aiden and I came in.

I met Ashley in her first year at Cobblestone. Ashley stuck out for a couple of reasons: she carried handbags that were ridiculously expensive even for Cobblestone, where the girls wore Tory Burch and Kate Spade, and she never went home—ever. Not even on weekends when the school let the students visit family.

So in November, I invited Ashley home for Thanksgiving. Scott tagged along.

I'm not sure how it happened exactly, but we absorbed the pair into our family. They began visiting for holidays; then once a month; and, eventually, every weekend. My father taught the pair how to drive when they turned sixteen, just as he taught Aiden and me.

My mom bought Scott his first guitar. Soon they became a regular staple in our lives.

I consider Ashley my sister, and I know Aiden views Scott as his brother. I can't say the same on that one.

I remember the exact moment when I realized it. My parents took us to Florida for the weekend for Ashley's sixteenth birthday—a rare treat, considering money was always tight. We stayed in a cottage by the ocean. Ashley and I were sitting in the sand, reading trashy magazines, when Scott walked out shirtless, and I temporarily forgot how to breathe. I even made a choking noise.

Somehow, I had never noticed how Scott's hips dipped into a little *V* at the bottom. Or how broad his shoulders were. Or that he had a white scar just under his shoulder blade.

That was when everything changed.

For me at least. I'm not an idiot. I know Scott still thinks of me as his little sister.

That is why even now, with him sitting so close to me and our shoulders hunched together, I know not to read too much into it. I bump his shoulder, and he grins. We are sitting in the boys' dressing room, sipping flavored bottled water. Across the room, Cole and Aiden are engaged in a dangerous game of air hockey, hooting and hollering every time they mash the plastic puck through. Kyle is warming up on the drums, and Ashley is watching with a dreamy expression.

I make a mental note to bring it up with her later.

"Carlz?" Scott looks at me quizzically. "You all right?"

"Hmm?"

"You made a weird sound."

"My feet are killing me." I scramble into a white lie. "From my heels last night."

"Your feet hurt?" Scott looks at me with his brow furrowed.

"Well, you try wearing heels to a restaurant, and let me know how your feet are the day after." I rush the words out.

"All right, all right." He holds his hands up in surrender. "Well? What do you think?"

I blink a few times. *God, his eyes are so green, almost like emeralds.* I blink a few more times and look down. He's showing me some sheet music. Of course it's probably good.

"It's good," I tell him with a shrug.

He gives me a dubious look. I let out a sigh and yank the paper out of his hands. I only need half a moment to study it to know it's different for him but in a good way.

"No, really. I know it isn't your usual style, but I like it." I trace a finger along the page, whistling the melody as I follow the notes. "I really like the second verse. There's something haunting about it."

"How do you do that?" he asks.

"What?" I pull a face. "Whistle?"

"No. I mean sound out the music like that."

"Oh. It's nothing. I've always been able to hear the music off the page." I feel my cheeks heating, and I curse my fair skin for the millionth time that evening for giving me away. "It's a hidden talent, I guess."

"How did I not know that about you?" Scott stares at me intently.

Before I have a chance to formulate a response, Kyle throws himself into the chair beside me and says, "Not bad, Carly." He grins. "Do you play an instrument?"

"Piano and guitar." I nervously twist my hands together, avoiding Scott's stare.

"A girl who's a fan of the classics. I like that." Kyle chuckles.

"But I'm not very good," I add maybe a bit too quickly. "Music is more Aiden's talent than mine."

"Don't lie to him," Scott says, gathering up the sheet music. "You're excellent on the guitar, Carly. You always have been."

I stare at him, firstly because it's unlike Scott to give compliments and secondly because he didn't call me Carlz. Something is clearly off here.

A knock on the door makes us all look up just as Julie peeks her head into the room. Her frizzy brown hair is secured in a knot on top of her head with a pen, and her clipboard is tucked tightly under her arm.

"Ten minutes, guys," she announces. "Scarlett is just about to wrap up her set."

At the sound of Scarlett's name, Ashley and I exchange a loaded glance. We haven't met Scarlett yet. She's Shade's opening act. I briefly noticed her at breakfast that morning, and the brief encounter over croissants and coffee was more than enough for a lifetime.

I want to like Scarlett. With her short blonde punk bob and signature ruby earrings, Scarlett is the coolest thing since Hydro Flasks.

But I found out as soon as Scarlett started berating the waiter this morning for bringing her cold coffee that she wasn't my cup of tea—or coffee.

"Oh, Julie." Aiden whistles, slinging an arm over her shoulders. "What would we do without you?"

She rolls her eyes. "Stop buttering me up, Aiden. You're not going out tonight."

"Not even one club?" His face falls.

"Not until the weekend." She purses her lips.

"But—"

"I'm the manager. Let me manage you," Julie says sternly with finality.

"You know," Aiden says, "you're kind of hot when you're bossy." He ruffles her hair.

I wait for Julie to sigh, roll her eyes, or say something rude, but to my surprise, she turns the same bubblegum pink as Scarlett's outfit.

Ashley and I exchange another glance.

Interesting.

"Time to go." Julie starts ushering the boys toward the stage entrance. "It's showtime."

We follow Julie to the holding area to the side of the stage and watch all four head out. The applause is deafening, running through the stadium like wildfire.

I must admit I tend to forget how talented my brother is. I watch Aiden's hands dance over the guitar strings. There's not a moment, though, to marvel before Kyle takes his seat behind the drums, and Cole picks up his bass. Then there's music.

I recognize the song even before Scott begins to sing.

> I shouldn't be here.
> I shouldn't be the one you call.
> Where there's trouble, there's me.
> 'Cause I don't think clear.
> I drop the ball.

My reputation precedes me.
If you want more talking,
baby, don't come knocking.
Just stop calling.

The crowd is going insane. The madness of it all is too much to take in. I blink, unable to process what I'm seeing.

Jesus.

OK, I'm not actually seeing Jesus. But with the way these girls are screaming and losing their minds, one would think Scott was sent down from heaven.

"Oh my God," Ashley whispers. Her eyes are suspiciously glassy. "They're really good, aren't they? I knew they would be, but to see it." She squeezes my hand. "Are you happy for them? I'm happy for them."

"I am," I choke out.

"They're idiots, but I love them."

"Me too." My eyes briefly catch Scott's, and he winks at me.

My throat feels tight as I watch him work the stage and crowd. Scott is a natural performer—he always has been—but I can tell when he messes up. It's not obvious to anyone else, but I know his nervous tics: the way he runs the back of his hand across his forehead when he's puzzled or the pulse that jumps in his jaw when he's angry at himself or nervous.

But why is Scott nervous? Is he trying to impress someone?

I suck in a sharp breath. Is he trying to impress me?

No. I shut the idea down as soon as it occurs to me. That is wishful thinking, and I'm not going to let myself go there. *Bad idea.*

As Shade strums the final chords, the crowd goes ballistic, jumping up and down as they roar their thunderous approval. All the guys pump fists with identical sweat-soaked shirts and looks of elated exhaustion.

I'm so damn proud of not just my brother but all four.

They come off the stage. Cole is first, and he picks Ashley up and twirls her around like a small doll as she laughs. Aiden and Kyle come off the stage next, slapping each other on the back.

Then there's Scott.

He comes off the stage last, cradling his guitar in his hands. He holds it gently, and I'm reminded of when we used to go snowboarding in Colorado while growing up. Scott would spend hours smoothing over his board with wax, patiently massaging out the cracks and lumps.

Scott's careful with the things he loves. He always has been.

"Scott!" I call out to him.

His head jerks up.

I beam a grin at him. "You were really—"

A squealing noise cuts me off.

"Baby!" a tall, sparkly brunette girl shrieks, hurrying toward them. "You were so good!"

She launches herself right into Scott's arms and kisses him squarely on the lips.

Chapter 5

This is the brunch from hell.

I push around my pancakes, drowning the flapjacks in a pool of syrup. Beside me, Ashley is on her third Bloody Mary of the morning—not because Ashley is hungover but because she must listen to Alissa speak.

I eye the girl in question.

There is nothing wrong with Alissa per se; in fact, if she would stop feeding Scott strawberries, I could grudgingly admit that I could probably like her. But there's something about her voice.

It's high-pitched and grating, like nails scratching across a chalkboard. I feel as if my ears are being slowly sandpapered off every time Alissa speaks.

OK, that's harsh and dramatic. But I'm allowed to be a little petty this morning, especially because this brunch was not my idea, and given the opportunity, I might strangle myself to death with one of the monogrammed napkins soon.

Next to me, Kyle shifts in his seat. "Whose idea was this brunch?" he whispers, as if reading my mind.

Inconspicuously, I tip my head toward Julie.

"Oh God, why would she do this to us?" Kyle groans.

"Apparently, team bonding."

"But Scarlett isn't here," he says.

"I know. Lucky her." I continue to mutilate my pancakes.

"Can't we just do a human knot?" Kyle arches an eyebrow at my display of animosity.

"Don't worry," I mutter. "I think Alissa already has that covered."

The girl in question is now sitting on Scott's lap with her arms wrapped around his neck in a way that I secretly find inappropriate for a ten o'clock brunch. I watch, horrified, as Alissa kisses Scott's neck. She has twisted around in a pretzel formation so that her body is facing the rest of us, but her head is fully facing Scott. I could have been impressed by her flexibility, but the sight makes me sick to my stomach.

Ashley takes one look at her brother and immediately signals a waiter. "Another drink, please," Ashley says, looking green. "Actually, make it a double. And please bring my friend a double as well." She points me out to the waiter, who nods in understanding.

"What did you say she does again?" I ask Ashley tightly.

"Backup dancer," Ashley says, taking a large swig of her next drink.

Of course. Right. That's it. I can't do this.

I look across the table and see that Aiden is playing a game on his phone, oblivious to the awkward tension in the room. Next to him, Cole is inhaling a huge stack of waffles without a care in the world, while Julie seems to be taking care of business on her tablet. This must be normal behavior from Scott.

Before I'm fully aware of what I'm doing, I scrape my chair back and rise to my feet. Seven pairs of eyes snap to look at me. I'm well aware that with my jean overalls and frizzy blonde hair, I probably have a shocking resemblance to someone right off a farm but not in a good way. I do not look cute in overalls.

"I need to go back to the hotel," I say tightly, and then I desperately attempt to back up my statement. "To lie down. I think I ate something bad yesterday."

"I can walk you back to the hotel." Immediately, Scott is full of concern.

That makes it worse because it's undoubtedly sisterly concern. He shifts Alissa off himself.

"No!" I half squeal.

Oh no, that is the very last thing I need: an extended conversation with Scott about his new girlfriend.

Scott ignores me and continues to collect his things.

"No, that's OK. It's only a five-minute walk," I say.

"I can use the fresh air," he replies.

"Oh, good." Aiden jumps in. "Can you two stop by the tailor on the way? I have a jacket I need to pick up."

"Actually, that would be so helpful, Carly." Julie looks up at me. "I have no idea how I'm going to get everything done today."

"Sure," I say lamely. "Not a problem."

"And get me some lemon juice?" Aiden's expression is hopeful. "For tonight's show?"

"You bet." Even though that is the last thing I want to do, I nod.

Aiden goes back to his bacon and eggs with gusto, looking pleased. Ashley looks as if she is coming up with plans to murder me via her plated breakfast.

"Don't you dare leave me with her," Ashley hisses, grasping my arm as I start to make my way past her. "Carly Taylor, I swear to God, if you take one step out of this restaurant—"

"See you back at the hotel, Ash." I kiss her on the cheek.

I hurry out of the restaurant, pulling on my light jean jacket and shoving my sunglasses on, hoping I can shake Scott. It still feels odd not to need a winter coat; in Colorado, going outside in December without a jacket is asking for frostbite. However, the blinding sunshine feels inappropriate for my current mood. I take a left at a cheerful candy shop, retracing our earlier steps. A group of girls on roller blades pass by, giggling and expressing excitement over the concert this evening.

"Do you think Scott will wear his leather jacket?"

"Oh my God, I hope so."

"And that Aiden—so dreamy."

"I'm more of a Cole girl myself, but I—"

Oh, please no. I can't take any more. I start scrambling in my pocket for my phone to dial Sophia.

"Carly! Wait up!"

Despite myself, I feel my heart lift. But as I turn around, I feel my heart squeeze. Scott still has lipstick marks on his neck. I grind my teeth. He jogs toward me; a baseball cap is pulled low over his face. He's carrying a takeout box that is leaking syrup.

"Pancakes," Scott says, offering it to me. "I thought you might want them later when you're feeling better."

Annoyingly, he's not even out of breath. Then I realize the gravity of the situation.

"What are you doing?" I hiss. "What if someone sees you—us?"

I glance around as if paparazzi or some crazy fans might jump out from behind any of the shops near the beach. And to be fair, they could; I've seen them hide in weirder places to get pictures of Aiden over the years. He once found them crammed in an Amazon box on his front porch.

"Why? Ashamed to be seen with me?" Scott grins. His voice is teasing, but there is something uncertain about it too, as if he's a little worried I might say yes.

"Of course not. I just don't think you want people to get the wrong idea if pictures get released of just the two of us," I say sort of lamely. Especially because he's used to being paired with Victoria's Secret models and French actresses. And now Alissa.

Admittedly, I don't think I'm bad looking, except for today's outfit, but I'm not particularly stunning either. I'm forgettable. And I'm OK with that—most of the time.

"Are you kidding me?" He stops in his tracks.

"I'm not." I suddenly actually feel sick.

"Carly don't be ridiculous," he says tightly. "C'mon. Let's get Aiden's stuff done and then go back to the hotel." He takes me by the elbow and starts guiding, half pulling me up the street.

We fall into step, and I decide to stop being so mad. It's just not worth it with this gorgeous weather. It's definitely not because he smells like wood smoke and vanilla. Absolutely not.

"So," I say as casually as possible, "how long have you been dating Alissa?"

"Not long." He shrugs casually. "And we aren't exactly dating."

My heart twists into a knot so tight it physically hurts. "And you like her?" I ask.

Unfortunately, he sees straight through my little charade. "Do you have a problem with her? Is there something you want to say?" he says equally tightly.

"It's just ..." I can't bring myself to say the words. "You and I grew up together. I care," I say lamely.

"Ah." His expression doesn't change.

"Forget it." I try to sound casual.

"Sure."

After that, we both seem careful to steer the conversation to anything but Alissa or relationships in general. We fall into an in-depth conversation about music, including some lyrics he's playing with. We tackle Aiden's requests, pausing to eat bits of the pancakes outside the shops. I'm surprised to realize I'm having fun.

Yes, that's the word: *fun*.

Astonishingly, Scott and I make it back to the hotel with only one group of girls noticing him. We navigate the shop and run out the back door before chaos erupts. Only when we are in the lobby do I realize our fingers are covered in sticky syrup. I look up at him and see he somehow has managed to get syrup on the tips of his hair sticking out under his hat, and I bite my lip to hide a smile.

"What is it?" he asks.

"It's—" I gesture to his hair. "You have some syrup."

Scott touches his hair with sticky fingers, compounding the problem, and I can't help but smile this time.

"I should shower," he says with a chuckle of his own.

"Me too." I laugh.

There's an awkwardly long pause, and my brain overanalyzes the situation.

"But not, like, together," I blurt out. "I mean in our separate rooms." My cheeks are on fire. "Obviously."

"Obviously," Scott repeats, grinning.

"So, I'll see you at the show later."

"Carlz!"

I'm halfway to the elevator when Scott calls out. I turn, and his smile grows uncertainly.

"I hope you're feeling better," he says.

"I think I am."

I take my time in the shower, using the cherry-scented hotel soap to scrub away all the sticky residue from the syrup. I shave my legs and lather my hair up. And just for the hell of it, I sing, because why not? Ashley isn't here. I turn the bathroom into my personal stage. What can it hurt?

I pick up the melody of a song I've been working on. It's upbeat, with lyrics that can touch the stars of heartbreak. I surprise myself to hear that it isn't terrible. It's not great, but it's not half bad—not that I'll ever share it with anyone.

After about fifteen minutes, I turn the water off and step out of the shower, pulling a fluffy white towel around my body.

I'm still humming as I walk out of the bathroom and into my room—where I nearly have a heart attack.

"Ah! Holy shit!" I scream, stumbling back a few feet.

Scott is lying comfortably on my bed, looking at me in amusement, clearly unfazed by my wearing only a towel.

"Scott!" I tug my towel tighter around myself. "You can't just break into people's rooms!"

"That's a good song," he says. "Who wrote it?"

"How the hell did you get in here?"

"Seriously," he said. "Anyone I know?"

"Seriously, how the hell did you get in here?" I repeat.

"Ashley gave me her key so I could come up and grab her purse. But forget that." He sits up. "Who wrote that?"

"You need to get out." *I'm going to kill Ashley.* I glare at him. "I'm serious, Scott."

I'm not sure how scary I look standing in front of him in a fluffy white towel and smelling of cherries, but Scott seems unfazed by my predicament.

"Be honest with me, Carly. Who wrote the song you were singing just now in the bathroom?" he says.

"Can you turn around?" I make a little spinning gesture with my finger. "I'm going to put some clothes on."

Scott's expression changes. It's as if he's only just now realized I'm only in a towel, and his gaze darts to my chest, where water droplets are pooling in my collarbones and dripping toward my stomach under my towel. His eyes go dark, the darkest I've ever seen. My mouth goes dry under his gaze.

"Yup," Scott says hoarsely. "Turning around." He turns and faces the opposite wall, with his spine stiff and straight.

I fumble blindly in my suitcase, cursing myself for not unpacking like Ashley, and grab the first things I find: jeans, a faded blue tank top, and white socks.

"Sorry about earlier," I mutter. "I didn't mean to upset you."

"I should have told you about Alissa."

"She seems nice." I yank on my jeans viciously.

"Yeah, she's …" He hesitates. "Well, she's Alissa."

For the second time today, there's a long, awkward pause between us.

Scott breaks it first. "Kyle seems to like you," he says. "He wouldn't shut up about you when we got back to the hotel room."

"Really?" I pause while tugging my tank top on.

"There's nothing going on between the two of you, right?"

"No," I say, which is 100 percent true. And anyway, it's none of Scott's business. "OK, you can turn around now."

Scott turns around slowly, as if he's bracing himself for the possibility that I'm lying and he's about to see me naked. I scowl at him, with my irritation rising to dangerous levels.

"You know, men have seen me naked."

"Carlz, I practically raised you," he says with a horrified expression.

I expect the words to sting, but I don't expect them to cut into my soul. I turn to the mirror, pretending to comb a knot out of my hair.

"You're right," I say flatly. "You're basically my brother." I'm half hoping he will flinch or show some sign that the words hurt him.

"Aiden certainly thinks so," he says in an unexpectedly equally flat tone.

"You should go," I tell him, mostly because if he spends a second longer lying on my bed and talking about how he is essentially a parent to me, I'm going to scream and claw out his eyes.

"I should." He gets up off my bed. "You'll stop by the dressing room before the show?" he asks.

He sounds so hopeful that even if I want to, I can't say no.

"Of course." I keep my eyes fixed on the mirror. It takes me a moment to realize that Scott is hovering near the door. I let out a sigh. "Is there something else?"

"I just realized. That song you were singing in the shower—you wrote it, didn't you?" He leans against the doorjamb.

I freeze with my hands midcomb in my hair. I catch Scott's eyes in the mirror, and I feel sucker punched in the gut.

Oh God. He knows.

I've never been good at hiding my feelings, especially not from Scott, and now my feelings are written across my face like music notes, easy to read and play with.

"Don't tell Aiden," I beg.

For a long moment, he looks at me. Then, with a sigh, he nods.

"You're incredibly talented, Carly," he tells me. "It's not Aiden's business."

He leaves me at a loss for words, closing my door behind him.

Chapter 6

Over the course of the next few weeks, I hardly get any productive sleep. We jet from city to city, visiting a new one practically every night, until the names become a blur. Ashley and I find different ways to entertain ourselves, such as doing touristy things and trying local cuisines.

By some miracle, Julie manages to keep us out of the papers, so we are free to roam around without fear of paparazzi. We have to worry only when Kyle joins us, which he does more and more frequently now. On the really bad jet-lag days, we spend a few hours by the hotel pool, or we just lie in bed, watching movies.

While we are lying in bed one day, Ashley says, "I love shopping just as much as the next girl, but I seriously miss sleeping."

"I don't know how the guys keep up with this schedule." I yawn so big my jaw makes a small popping sound.

A knock comes on our room door.

"If that's Kyle, tell him this is not a shopping day. I need at least ten more hours of sleep before I can function normally again." Ashley groans from under her covers.

I roll my eyes as I pry myself out of my bed and pad my way across the floor, avoiding a tipped-over trash can, suitcases, shoes, and bags. I use the tiny peephole in the door to confirm that it is, in fact, Kyle. I rub my eyes viciously and smooth my shirt down before I open the door to him.

"Are you ladies looking to get out today? We are in the Sunshine

State, after all," Kyle says cheerfully as he pushes past me into our room.

His cheeriness makes me want to punch him in the face, but instead, I follow him back inside.

"Kyle, no offense, but how are you awake and already on the go? We just checked in like six hours ago. Don't you sleep?" I finish my rant by face-planting back into my bed.

"Been used to this type of schedule for months now. Scott basically put me through a pretend tour schedule as part of my interview process for the band. If I succeeded without falling on my face, I was in. So here I am." He gestures to himself proudly.

"Well, we aren't adjusted. We need sleep. There's no concert tonight, so this is my complete sleep day," Ashley snaps from under her covers.

I open one eye to see Kyle's smile fade as he takes in the state of us. "Kyle, what are the other guys doing? Don't you need to hang out with them?" I ask him in a kinder and softer tone.

He shrugs. "The guys don't care. Aiden and Cole always end up playing video games or finding some kind of arcade that is Julie-approved. Scott has just been putting himself in a bubble of solitude, it seems. In other words, he doesn't want company."

There is much in his explanation that needs to be unboxed, but my exhausted brain is only working on two power cells, so I only catch the last part about Scott.

"Is Scott OK?" I ask him.

"He seems to be," Kyle says with a shrug. "Are you ladies sure about staying in?"

I'm too busy trying to get my brain to process the fact that Scott seems to be fine with Alissa to reply. Ashley's brain, however, must be working better.

"Kyle, we love you, and we want you to have fun, but please let us sleep," she whines.

"OK, OK, I'll let you two get back to sleep. If anyone asks, I'll be down at the beach. My mum will kill me if I don't send her some photos of the famous Sunshine State." He gives a pitiful look before heading out and closing the door behind him.

I've noticed that Kyle calls his mom a lot, probably at least once a day, and every time, I get a pang of hot jealousy.

If only I were that close with my parents. I call them once a week, but it's mostly out of a misplaced sense of duty. Aiden never calls them, so it falls on me to keep in touch while I'm here. Pretty much every phone call is the same: they pepper me with questions about my returning to school so I can still join Dad at his firm and ask how Scott and Aiden are, if the fans are still crazy, and how the new drummer is. My answers are always the same: not going to happen, fine, always crazy, and fantastic.

I end up seeing little of Scott in the following days, but that might be because I'm doing my best to avoid him. Where there's Scott, there's Alissa, and Alissa seems to think it's her sworn duty to cover as much of his surface area with her skin as possible. It's nauseating. Ashley and I both get sick just thinking about it—but for different reasons.

"I mean, he's my brother," Ashley gripes as we wipe gloopy green masks off our faces at a hotel in New Jersey. "It's disgusting."

"I know," I tell her.

"I can never look my own brother in the eye again." Ashley wets her washcloth. "If I never have to see him with another girl again, it'll be too soon."

"I hear you."

"And it must be even worse for you since you're in love with him."

"Yeah, it's—" I freeze, swinging around to look at her. "Wait. What did you just say?"

"Well, you are, aren't you?" Ashley arches an eyebrow expectantly at me.

I busy myself with my own washcloth, unable to meet her eyes. I always suspected Ashley knew about my crush on Scott, but to hear her say the words is like having an entire bottle of narcotics emptied into my bloodstream.

"It doesn't matter," I reply, wringing the washcloth. "He's with Alissa."

"I think that's about run its course." She snorts.

"And then there's you. And Aiden."

"Oh, we don't care," Ashley says with a wave of a hand. She pauses. "Well, Aiden might, actually. But we can deal with that later."

"And Scott is ..." I trail off, scrubbing at a bit of face mask under my chin.

"He's what?" Ashley crosses her arms and meets my eyes in the mirror.

I bite my lip. How can I tell her about my fears? How I'm terrified Scott will flat-out reject me? How I'm afraid he doesn't want to have a serious committed relationship?

Ashley is his sister.

"He's too tall for me," I say, chickening out of the truth.

"Don't worry," she says with pursed lips. "We'll get you a step stool."

"Ashley!" I just stare at her with my eyes wide.

"I've known for years." She sighs and sits down. "I just wish he would stop screwing around and come clean to you." She rubs her hands over her now-smooth cheeks. "I've been planning your wedding for like at least five years."

"What are you talking about?" Either my brain has turned completely off, or I'm still reeling from the turn this conversation has taken.

"He's in love with you, Carly." She slumps down to the bathroom floor. "Has been for ages. Hell, most of his lyrics are about you." She suddenly looks incredibly exhausted again.

"Wait, Ashley. Rewind, and freeze." I slide down to the floor next to her. "What are you saying?"

She reaches over and grabs my hand. "I'm saying, as his sister who wants to toss him out a twenty-story window half the time, please do not give up on him."

I sit frozen in shock. Everything feels as if it's changed, yet nothing has changed. I've never picked up the impression that my feelings could be reciprocated.

"OK. I won't give up on him." I reach over and pull her into a hug to comfort both of us.

⟫◆⟪

On April 7, all of us fly out of New York. To my relief, Alissa is flying back to Hawaii to visit her parents for the Easter weekend. I'm disappointed that Cole and Kyle are leaving as well for about a week, but I don't hold it against them for wanting to spend time with their families over Easter weekend.

"I'll bring you back some Aussie treats," Kyle tells me. "You'll love them."

"Should I be worried?" I playfully slap his arm.

"You'll have to wait and see." He grins.

Kyle kisses me on the cheek before he heads off for his flight, and I notice Scott watching me. His expression is unreadable. He only relaxes when the rest of us are all on the private jet, munching on some pretzels and peanuts, as our plane speeds toward Colorado. Home.

"So," Scott says, "who's up for some hometown barhopping?"

Ashley and I eagerly express excitement in unison.

"I wish I could," Julie says, sounding genuinely disappointed. "I'm meeting an old friend for a drink." Her eyes dart among the four of us. "You're all welcome to join us if you'd like, though," she adds.

"Well, I can't go," Aiden says, stretching out his legs. "I have a date."

Silence descends on us before the explosion.

"You have a what?" I ask.

At the same time, Ashley screeches, "Who is she?"

"I told you not to say anything, buddy." Scott sighs.

I whip around to stare at him. "You know about this?"

"Yes, I've known for a few days," Scott says nervously.

"And you didn't think to mention it?"

"I haven't seen much of you," Scott says. He speaks so quietly that I almost miss it. The others on the plane seemingly do.

"You have a date?" Julie says. "Aiden, do we know her?"

It doesn't look as if she thinks it's wonderful. In fact, Julie looks as if she is two seconds away from opening the escape hatch and leaping out of the plane. Her hands are tightening convulsively on thin air, as if she is itching to clench her clipboard.

Aiden notices this too. "Don't worry, Julie," he says, grinning. "You don't need to pencil it into our schedule or anything."

"Funny," Julie says with a maniacal laugh.

"Do I know her?" Ashley asks, seemingly oblivious to Julie's inner turmoil. "Is she another backup dancer?"

Oh Lord, I hope not.

"No," Aiden says smugly. "It's Scarlett."

Everyone goes silent.

"Not, like, the Scarlett we know, though?" I ask hopefully. "Some other Scarlett."

Aiden stares at me. "Yes, of course it's the Scarlett you met. How many Scarletts do you think I know?"

"Well, I just …" I trail off.

"Aiden, you have to give me a heads-up on some of this, at least from a PR perspective." Julie practically growls at him.

"Her plane should arrive in a few hours. I invited her out here for the weekend," he says with a hint of finality.

"Oh no." Ashley groans, abandoning all pretenses. "You're dating your opening act? Aiden, she's awful. I caught her shouting at her manager the other day."

"She was probably having a bad day," he says defensively.

"She called him an incompetent rat." She presses meaningfully. "And then fired him. I don't think it was just a bad day."

"Well, I like her," Aiden says firmly. "So the rest of you will just have to deal with it."

With that, Aiden slumps back in his seat, sticking headphones in ears.

Mercifully, not long after that, we start to descend into Denver, so we don't have a whole lot of time to stew in the awkward silence.

I'm not even completely off the plane before I see Aiden climb into his own separate car. I watch as it speeds away as I wobble down the rest of the steps in my boots and drag my suitcase toward the only other remaining car. Julie, a few paces behind me, is uncharacteristically quiet. She and I shove our luggage into the trunk and climb inside, where the driver has the heat on full blast.

"Right," Scott says, breathing into his black gloves for warmth. "Where to?" he asks as he and Ashley climb in, making me grateful that this SUV seems to be oversized.

"Here." Julie hands the driver an address on a piece of paper. "Just drop me off first so these crazy hooligans can go wherever," she says with exhaustion laced through her words. "Just don't get into any real trouble," she tells us sternly.

"You got it." The driver nods in acknowledgment and pulls the car out of the airport.

It's a quiet twenty-minute drive with minimal traffic to the location Julie has requested. We pull up to a massive, modern three-story house.

"Julie, whose house is this?" I can't stop the words from tumbling out.

"An old friend of mine. Her husband is away on business, so I'm really doing her a favor by keeping her company these next few days." She gives a reassuring smile before climbing out.

The driver deftly pulls out her luggage and takes it up to the door for her. With a tip of his hat, he rejoins us in the warmth.

"Where to next?" he asks casually but professionally.

"Actually," Ashley says, "I don't feel very well."

"What?" I frown at her as concern takes precedence over anything. "Is it a headache?"

Ashley shakes her head. "My stomach. I think I ate too many pretzels."

"But you only had two small packages." I furrow my brow with more concern.

"Maybe it was the plane ride then."

"Well, I'll go home with you," I tell her, having visions of Ashley clinging to a toilet bowl as she hacks up bits of pretzels. "We can watch a movie instead. Scott, you don't mind if we—"

"No!" Ashley practically shouts. "You and Scott go out. I'll be fine on my own."

Then, too late, it all makes sense, and I understand what she is doing. Ashley isn't sick, the little liar. She's probably going to binge on ice cream and watch a marathon of one of her favorite TV dramas. I glare at her, and she smiles back, the picture of innocence.

"I'll be OK," Ashley says. "You two have fun."

"Are you sure, Ash?" Scott looks torn, with his older-brother instincts firing into overdrive. "What if you need to go to the hospital?"

"I'll call you." She waves him off.

"Leave your ringer on," he says. "I'll check in."

And just like that, Scott and I get left outside a local bar and grill while Ashley heads to her place. For the first time in days, Scott and I are left alone together. I fidget with my hands while I wait for him to say something—anything—since I don't know what to say. What the hell do we normally talk about when we are alone? Music? Our families?

Thankfully, he speaks up.

"Let's go inside and grab a table. It's freezing."

He takes a few steps toward the door and yanks it open, not checking to see if I follow him through. I do follow him inside and toward the bar area. Scott slides into a high-top and yanks his ball cap off. I take the seat across from him and feel obvious anger rolling off him. An innocent young woman at a nearby table spills her drink when she sees Scott.

"You don't need to worry about Aiden, you know?" he says. "I don't think he's that serious about Scarlett."

I almost laugh out loud. He thinks I'm worried about my brother going on a date right now. He couldn't be further from the truth. I use it as a cop-out, though.

"I just wish he'd date someone nice," I say.

"Like who?"

"Like Julie. Or even Ashley," I say before I can filter my words.

"What on earth are you talking about? Both of those options are off-limits." He looks at me as if I've grown a second head or a pair of tentacles.

"And why's that?" I scoff at him. "Is there a rule or something? That you guys can only date mean girls?" I fold my arms with frustration building like a fire inside me. I'm treading in dangerous waters here.

"No, because Julie is our manager, and Ashley is my sister." He aggressively stuffs his hands into his pockets.

I know he's not immune or stupid, but his next set of actions leaves me room to worry. I watch, glued to my chair, as he walks up to one of the bartenders. I can't hear what he's saying, but I watch emotions from recognition to glee to fear cross the young man's face. Scott slips him some bills on the counter, and as if on cue, the young man climbs up onto the bar to address the room in its entirety.

"This young man here has asked to be left alone." He gestures to Scott. "We all know who he is, and he has asked for total privacy for the evening. In exchange, he will cover everyone's tab this evening!"

Nobody moves or makes a sound.

"Everyone got that?" the bartender shouts.

After a few acknowledge and a few give salutes toward Scott, the bartender climbs down and hands Scott a prefilled bucket of ice with twelve beers in it. Scott comes back to the high-top table with a look of satisfaction on his face and slides back into his chair. The ice-filled bucket makes a thud as he plops it down on the table between us. I pop the top of a beer and take a long swig.

"You must miss her," I finally say with the same compulsive, masochistic tendency as a person picking at a scab to watch it bleed. "I'm surprised you didn't fly out to Hawaii with her."

Scott frowns, as if the idea hasn't even occurred to him. "I wanted to spend the weekend with you," he says. He then adds quickly, "All of you. Ashley and Aiden too." His smile is a flash in the darkness. "It'll be like old times."

My heart sinks. *Old times.* So that's what this is to Scott. I know this isn't a date, and I know Ashley was supposed to be here as well, but I didn't think we'd be reliving our childhood. I sit back in my seat and take it all in. Here we are, back home for the first time in months for me and even longer for him, and we are sitting in a bar. I almost laugh out loud, but a brilliant idea comes to mind.

"You want to get out of here?" I finish off my beer and start to get up.

"And go where?" he asks with humor in his tone.

There's nothing here but beer, mountains, and cold air.

"I think that's the root of tonight's problem." I zip my coat up.

"I wasn't aware of any problem." He raises his eyebrows at me but starts to gather his things.

"I think you need to reacquaint yourself with your roots," I say a little too aggressively as I yank on my gloves.

"Oh? What exactly do you have in mind?" he says with a grin.

"Snowboarding," I say. I watch as his grin disappears.

"Excuse me?" Scott asks urgently as I pull him out the door. "You can't be serious." He pulls me to a stop by my elbow.

"Yes." I yank my elbow free. "I'm totally serious."

"Carly," Scott says, sounding more worried as I start walking in the direction of Ashley's apartment, "what are you doing?"

"Ashley's place." I shrug and keep walking. "It's only a couple blocks from here. We can grab our gear from her storage shed and borrow her truck to get up the mountain."

The shock on Scott's face is so priceless that I can't help but laugh. I'm not sure which he is more surprised by: that I'm taking the lead for once or that I'm suggesting we go snowboarding at night.

"Listen, we aren't going to actually go down the mountain. They have indoor skiing and snowboarding now." I roll my eyes at his silence.

"Oh? I didn't know that. It's been a while," he says solemnly.

"It has. Plus, this indoor place is just a baby version. If you break any part of yourself, Julie will kill me," I say as we round the corner.

"You'd better not let me break anything then." He chuckles.

———◦◦◦———

The indoor facility is pretty busy for this time of night. I'm not the only one who had this great idea this evening. A combination of rock and pop music blares out of the speakers overhead, and the smell of hot chocolate is ripe in the air. Scott pulls his hood farther down over his face as he looks nervously around. But everyone is so busy with his or her tricks and skills that nobody even looks twice at us. I smile smugly as I pass him his board.

"Let's see how much you remember," I say a bit tauntingly.

"How uncharacteristically sadistic of you." He raises his eyebrows at me.

"I learn from the best."

"I assume you mean Ashley."

"Well, yes." I playfully swat him on the shoulder. "But you as well."

We strap on our gear and head to the top of the inside man-made mountain. Embarrassingly, I stumble a few times, and Scott reaches out to grip my arm, steadying me. I can feel the warmth of his hand even through my multiple layers. I can't help but shiver slightly at his touch. Scott frowns down at me.

"Here," he says, wrapping his scarf around my neck. "It's bloody freezing in here."

I decide not to correct him.

We get to the top and plant our boards side by side, plotting our course for the way down. I glance over at Scott to see if he's having any second doubts, and I'm pleasantly surprised to see pure excitement on his face.

"Take this round slow and easy? Or race?" I ask him, thinking I already know the answer.

"Carly Taylor, we are definitely racing," he says as he places his eye mask over his eyes.

"Good. See you at the bottom!" I tip my board forward and take off.

We weave side to side down the hill for a few seconds before I see Scott start to fall into his old rhythm. I slow myself down so I can watch him take a ramp at speed and do a 360 spin before landing straight on and zooming away. My heart practically zooms away with him. I bend my knees low and lean forward to pick up speed, but he's already at the bottom, grinning like an idiot, and for that grin, this is an absolute success.

"How'd that feel?" I ask him as I glide to a stop in front of him.

"Like a breath of fresh air." He bends and picks up his board. "I forgot how free that feels."

"It's good to know that you can still ride like a pro." I chuckle as I bend down, unstrap my feet, and clumsily step out. I start heading back toward the path to go again and realize he isn't right behind me.

I turn around and see him staring at me with a strange expression on his face, as if he has just realized something. I fidget with my board a little nervously.

"Scott?" I say with uncertainty in my voice.

"Sorry." He shakes his head as if to clear it. "I was lost in thought."

"What about?"

"I was thinking …" He hesitates and then grins. "I was just thinking that you should actually race this time. Instead of letting me win."

I can tell by the look in his eyes and the way his smile isn't quite right that he isn't telling me the truth. In fact, this is probably the first time he's ever outright lied to my face.

<hr/>

The next morning comes too soon. Since it is Easter Sunday, I feel it wouldn't be appropriate to avoid my parents. That is how I end up sitting at the dining room table with Aiden next to me and our parents across from us. Thankfully, Aiden has told Scarlett she can skip this wonderful family occasion.

"What do you mean you're going back with Aiden?" My dad slams a fist down on the table.

"I mean just that." I cross my arms. "I already told you that I'm not going back to university right now." I shoot him a glare.

"C'mon, Dad. Ease up. Carly is a huge help on tour." Aiden squeezes my hand under the table. "It's actually beneficial in multiple ways for Carly to come out and finish this tour with us."

"Is that so?" Our mom shoots daggers at the pair of us.

"Yes." Aiden runs a hand through his hair in frustration. "So leave it alone. She's coming back with me."

Chapter 7

A knock at my hotel room door startles me. I'm in the kitchen in my suite. I love baking and find it relaxing, especially today, of all days. I dust off the flour from my hands before opening the door. I swing the door open and receive an assortment of flowers and boxes of chocolates thrust into my face.

"Surprise!" Aiden shouts proudly.

Leave it to my brother to go a little overboard.

"Oh, Aiden." I gasp as my cheeks turn pink. "You shouldn't have!"

"Happy birthday, Carlz." He grins like a lunatic. "I can't believe you're twenty-three now!" he exclaims excitedly.

"I can't believe you remembered!" I squeal as I launch myself at him, tackling him in a hug. It's uncommon for Aiden to remember anyone's birthday besides his own.

"With a little reminder from multiple anonymous sources," he admits with a sigh. "But seriously, I've got lunch reservations for us at the Beaumont." He puffs his chest out a bit proudly.

"OK!" I clap in excitement. "I'll change fast and be ready to go."

After I change outfits twice, the driver takes three wrong turns, and the hostess loses her ability to speak upon laying her eyes on Aiden, we finally sit down to order. I look around and take in the delicious smells and modern decor, which are the opposite of most of the Texas restaurants we've been to. Other than the restaurant I went to in Los Angeles, it's the nicest place I've been while on tour with the guys. The manicured greenery that dangles down from the ceiling and the white napkins, which are crisp and ironed, add a touch of simple elegance. The air smells divine, like olive oil and freshly cooked bread. It's easily the best lunch spot Aiden, or whoever helped him, could have picked.

I sip my water while I weigh the pros and cons of telling my brother about the handful of finished songs I currently have hidden at the bottom of my suitcase. Scott's reaction the day he heard me singing in the bathroom put the itch of excitement in me again over my music. The only problem is Aiden. Music is his thing—to him and our parents.

Our first course of salad and bread arrives, and I decide to just take the plunge. After all, it is my birthday, and that automatically puts good vibes in everything today. I look across the table, where Aiden is digging into his salad with enthusiasm.

"You didn't have to do this, you know," I tell him as I stab at a piece of lettuce. "I'd have been happy with going to a barbecue food truck."

"This is better," he says around a mouthful of bread.

"Still." I lean forward, taking the extra piece of bread off his plate. "Thanks, Aid."

I pop the fresh bread into my mouth, savoring the taste of the cinnamon butter. *God, the only thing that could make it taste better is if Scott—*

I stop the train of thought in its tracks. *No.*

Immediately, I feel guilty. Here I am, enjoying a nice birthday lunch with my brother. I shouldn't be thinking about Scott and his abs.

Unfortunately, Aiden's next topic of conversation isn't much better.

"So," he says after placing his empty salad bowl to the side, "college."

I almost choke on my bite of salad. "Do we have to talk about this right now?" I groan.

"You can't put it off forever," Aiden says.

If I were more like Ashley, I would tell my brother to shove it. As it is, I merely take a delicate sip of water.

"There's nothing to discuss," I say as firmly as I can. "I'm not going back to economics, Aiden. I mean it." I cross my arms in defense.

"Then what do you want to do?"

My grip tightens on my fork. Instinctively, I want to lie to him—to tell him I don't know or to come up with something else, like joining the Peace Corps—but then I remember Scott's face when he overheard me singing in the shower.

What was it he said? Oh, right. "You're incredibly talented, Carly. It's not Aiden's business."

"Do you remember my first talent show?" I ask him abruptly. "The one I did in sixth grade in front of the whole school?"

"Yes. Why?" He blinks confusedly at me.

"You and Scott did a surprise performance in the form of a country song," I say, ignoring him. "You wore cowboy boots and everything, remember?"

"And a hat," he adds, grinning. "God, I was terrible at the guitar."

"And me?" I say. "Do you remember what I did?"

Aiden screws up his face, and even though I expected it, even though I knew he wouldn't remember, it still feels like a blow.

"It was an original piece," I say.

"Carlz, is there some reason you're bringing this up?" He runs a hand through his hair, a sign that he's getting stressed out.

I clasp my hands tightly under the table. I want to shake Aiden. I want to scream into his face until he understands, until he gets what I'm trying to say to him.

But I don't do any of that.

"Well, I've never stopped writing." I wait for a beat to see if he reacts.

He goes chillingly still like a statue.

I press forward. "I've got a handful of finished songs I would love to share with you and maybe get your feedback on." I clumsily trip over my words, trying to get them all out.

"What then?" Aiden asks so quietly I almost don't hear him.

"I don't know," I say honestly.

"Was this all part of a plan? To drop out of college, get me to let you come on tour with me, and then use me like a stepping-stone to get to one of the label producers? Over what? Some poetry you have scribbled in a diary?" His tone and words are like a cold slap across my face.

"What on earth are you talking about?" I whisper-shout back at him. "None of that is true! You know that." I feel tears prick my eyes.

"Oh? It all seems pretty convenient to me," he says with frostbite in his words.

"You clearly don't know anything about me, Aiden Taylor. Your own sister." I get up from the table and gather my things. "I won't be at tonight's concert."

I rush out of the restaurant, knowing I'm seconds away from a waterfall of tears. *So much for that going well.*

Once I'm outside and down the block, I find myself in a small, fairly quiet park. I find a bench that's hidden from the street, under one of the trees, and fumble for my phone as I sit down. My whole body feels numb over what just happened. How on earth could he think that of me?

I mentally run down the list of whom I can call for a ride. Ashley? Cole? Kyle? Scott? Julie? I decide to try Cole first. He's the one least likely to ask questions. Unsurprisingly, though, his phone goes straight to voice mail. He's probably getting his hair styled for tonight.

I'm not sure why Kyle is my next choice, but I find myself listening to the ringing sound. Unlike Cole, Kyle picks up.

"Carly?" He says my name as a question.

"Kyle, I need a ride," I tell him as I choke back a sob.

"Where's Aiden? Aren't you at lunch with him?" he asks in a concerned voice.

"Kyle, please. Just come get me. I'll text you my location," I beg.

"I'm on my way," he says before I end the call.

I text him my location and sit and wait.

The car ride back to the hotel is nothing short of deafening silence. Kyle doesn't ask questions, and I don't offer up any kind of answers or explanations. We manage to get inside the hotel and up to my room without exchanging many words at all. I fumble with my key card and end up dropping it. He bends down, snags it, and swiftly unlocks the door in the same fluid motion. He doesn't ask, and I won't stop him from following me inside.

"Um, do you want a drink or something?" I lamely offer while I wring my hands in front of me for something to do besides crying.

"Cut the crap, Carly. You don't have to go into the details, but are you OK?" he says matter-of-factly as he leans against the wall.

"No, I'm not," I stutter, choking on sobs and almost falling to the floor. He catches me and slowly moves me to the couch.

"Where's Ashley? Should I find her?" he asks as I work to calm myself down.

"No!" I shout louder than I intend to. "Please. This is the kind of fight you don't drag others into." I recover with a wave of my hand.

"Carly, what happened between you and Aiden at lunch?" he asks softly and somberly.

"We just don't see certain things the same way—that's all," I answer cryptically through my tears. I can't help but think to myself that it never goes well when bandmates start picking sides that aren't each other.

"Is this about music?" he asks as he runs a hand through his hair. "It's always about music with Aiden," he adds upon seeing my questioning look.

"You're not wrong," I say sadly. "It's always about music with Aiden." I press my eyes to stop the tears.

"I heard you playing around on the guitar with Scott that day before our show." He shoves his hands into his pockets. "Is this about you having talent? Or about you finally wanting to do something with it?" he asks in a soft tone.

"You're pretty observant." I let out a sigh. "Honestly, probably both," I tell him.

"I see." He doesn't move; he just looks around, and I watch as his eyes land on the song journal I left out on the table. "Is that what I think it is?" he asks with a mischievous smile.

"Uh …" Not sure what to say, I start inching toward it in the hope of shoving it out of sight.

I'm a half step too late, as he lunges forward, snatches the little book off the table, and flips it open.

"Give that back." I reach for the notebook, but he bounces back and grins.

"Is this the famous songbook Ashley has mentioned to me?" He holds it teasingly above my reach.

"Kyle, please." I panic.

"Let me read some," he says with a pout.

"Fine." I let out a groan and flop down into the nearest chair.

He flips through the pages until he settles on one. His brows knit together as his eyes dart across the page.

"Causes nothin' but late-night cries," he murmurs.

"Damn it, Kyle, just hand it over." My heart hammers as I leap off the chair.

"Those lyrics are beautiful. I wish you'd play them." He snaps the book shut and passes it to me.

"I can't." I hug the notebook to my chest and stare at the ground.

"Because of Aiden?" He almost spits.

"Music is his thing," I say with a shrug.

"Which is the dumbest thing I've heard since being here in America." He shakes his head disappointedly. "Carly." He sighs. "If you learn anything from being on tour with us, it's that you should take a risk once in a while. Wishing for something won't make it happen." He shoves his hands back into his pockets.

"Kyle—"

He quickly interrupts me. "Listen, Aiden is great. His music is great. But so are you. So is yours. Music isn't exclusive to your brother because he has a band and you don't."

"You sound a lot like Ashley now." I let out a long breath.

"She's wise." He smiles.

"Mhmm." I smile back at him.

He looks at his phone and sighs. "It's getting late in the afternoon. I should start heading to the arena." He starts shuffling toward the door.

"Good luck tonight! I'm sure I'll see you tomorrow."

"You're not coming tonight?" He looks almost disappointed.

"No, Aiden and I need a day or two of space," I say sadly.

"Makes sense." He shrugs. "If you ever want someone to listen to your music, you know I'm here for you."

"Thanks." I walk over and hug him.

"Also, happy birthday, Carly," he says with a small smile.

"Thanks." I grin up at him.

I pull away, and he heads out without looking back. The door latches softly behind him.

Once he's gone, an idea clicks on in my head like a lightbulb. Despite Aiden's harsh words, I need to make it of my own accord with my music. I need to stop being a coward with my head stuck in the damn clouds. I need to be brave, to be fearless.

I dig out my laptop and place it in front of me on the bed. After it boots up, I click around for a moment before opening the video-recording program. The red recording button stares me down, and I hover the cursor over the Close button. *What am I thinking?*

"Be fearless," I mutter to myself.

I grab my guitar and hit the Record button. *Recording* flashes in red, and my entire body freezes. I hit the Stop button and lay the guitar down next to me.

"Carly," I grumble, "you need to do this. You have to."

I restart the recording and take a deep breath. *I can do this. I am cool, calm, and confident. Because I, Carly Taylor, am going to do this. This isn't about my parents or Aiden. This is about me.*

I strum the chords, and a soft melody hums around me. As I dive into the music, the nerves float away. When I hit the lyrics, I open my mouth and force the words out.

> I know you tell the world lies,
> but all I need is for you to try.
> I can't sit, can't stand, can't wait.
> You always take all these girls' bait.

I pause.

> I place your voice in the background.
> Just to turn my frown upside down.
> But lately, just lookin' in your eyes
> causes nothin' but late-night cries.

I don't realize I've finished the entire song until my eyes focus on the blinking light. I end the recording and put my guitar down. I hit the Play button and cringe at the sight of my face.

Come on—what is my face doing? Why are there so many wrinkles? I look like I'm being tortured by something. Ugh. I can never show this video, let alone post it anywhere—not with my face in it at least.

My phone vibrates, signaling a text message, and I open it to read it. The message is from Scott: "Happy birthday, Carly." There's an attachment of a bunch of people cheering and going crazy with balloons. He probably grabbed it from the internet. But it makes me smile nevertheless.

"Thanks. You're the best," I type back.

My eyes land on Ashley's costume makeup sitting on the dresser, and I smile. For once, I think Ashley's decision to bring the makeup is genius. I scramble off the bed, collect it all, and head to the bathroom. I've helped Ashley a few times in the past with her costume makeup, so I'm fairly familiar with the items she has.

I use the makeup to transform my face, using vibrant purples and pinks as eye shadow and glitter to accent my eyes. I even place small diamonds under my eyes for a more drastic change. After I paint my lips a rich dark red, I outline my lips with small diamonds as well. I tap a whole brushful of glitter across my cheeks and use finishing spray to help it all stick in place. I frizz out my hair and methodically style it in a way I normally don't wear it.

Last but not least, I grab one of Ashley's glittery tops I normally wouldn't wear myself and change my shirt.

I step back from the mirror and examine my reflection.

If I didn't know it's my own reflection, I wouldn't recognize myself.

The video only shows me from the waist up, so this is all the transformation I need. I return to my computer and settle in front of it with my guitar. I take a deep breath and start again.

This time, the girl in the video radiates confidence and talent. She isn't afraid of the world or what people might say. I wish I could be her without makeup. Maybe one day I will be. I open YouTube, and there are suggestions of other people singing. Their videos have tons of views and lovely comments from users. I wish that were me. Scott's voice dances through my mind: *"You're incredibly talented, Carly."*

I decide to stop wishing and to do something. Somehow, I click on the Upload Video button and select the file. My entire body vibrates as it uploads. I can still back out of this. What if people don't like my voice or the song? What if they leave negative comments? What if nobody cares to watch the video? I'm not sure which alternative is the worst. The video finishes, and my heart just about explodes. I jump up and pace the length of my room.

I could post the video and delete it after twenty-four hours. That's kind of brave, right? Or I could delete everything and go back to my safe little bubble, wishing I was one of those girls.

I take a deep breath, hit Publish, and close my eyes. The page reloads, and I quickly exit it.

Chapter 8

Morning seems to come all too quickly. I push the thought of checking my computer out of my head. I could have one view or one thousand; it all feels pretty far-fetched. The fact that I spent the night dreaming about the bright lights of a stage and a crowd roaring my name as I belt out my songs has nothing to do with today's agenda.

There's a soft knock on the door, and then Ashley pokes her head into the room. I snuggle deeper under the blankets.

"We're leaving in an hour. Will you be ready by then?" she asks.

"Um, yes." I nod. "Because I really don't have another choice, do I?"

"Don't forget to eat breakfast," she says. "We don't have any time on our layover today to grab any decent food."

"OK," I say.

She closes the door while I roll out of bed.

Waking up is the easy part; fighting the desire to roll back into bed and ignore the world is the hardest. I stumble across the room and begin stuffing my suitcase back together. After grabbing a pair of clean sweatpants and a hoodie, I quickly get changed for the day of travel. I step into the bathroom and yank a brush through my hair before throwing it up into a messy updo.

Once I have all my things together, I wander into the hallway of the hotel and instantly groan with displeasure when I hear my brother's yelling coming from down the hall, from a different room.

"Not my problem," I mutter to myself.

My feet drag along the ground as I take the elevator down to the lobby. I look around and don't see anyone else down here yet, so I pull out my phone and start scrolling through posts and news articles while I polish off a couple of granola bars I snagged from the room.

A nearby television has a morning show on, and I watch as the two anchors appear on the screen as the perfect examples of fake and dramatic. For the most part, I tune it all out as I continue scrolling through different news articles on my phone.

"Last night, a video of a young girl singing went viral, erupting a brand-new audience going crazy for this girl's song and voice."

I snap my attention to the television in the lobby and tune in to what they are talking about. My mind refuses to put two and two together. I look down at my phone and see different articles reporting on the same story pop up on my newsfeed. When I see a still picture someone grabbed from the video in question, my heart falls up and out of my throat.

I quickly rush over to one of the lobby computers and sign in to the internet. I pull up YouTube and wait for it to load. Once it does, I'm speechless. Right in front of me, clear as day, is my video, with millions of views and thousands of comments. I quickly close out of all the browsers and log off the computer before sinking into one of the cushy chairs in the lobby.

"Well, good morning, sunshine. Missed you last night." Cole appears out of nowhere and plops down next to me.

"Hi, Cole," I mutter with my eyes still closed.

"Have you heard about that new internet singer? I already love her after one song." He beams with excitement.

I slowly open my eyes and look over at him. I must seem as if I'm hungover, because I can't seem to put words together.

"What's wrong with Aiden this morning? I heard him yelling down the hall," I say.

"Probably having a diva moment. We were all woken up by the record label this morning, about the girl who's going viral from the video." He shrugs as if it's no big deal.

"Really? How come?" I can't seem to stop myself.

"Well, the account owner has Colorado tagged as a home location. And we are all from Colorado, so of course, they think we all must know who she is." He shrugs again.

I feel all the color drain out of my face. Colorado is my home location, which is why the location on the account is marked as such.

"You know, I don't think I've seen the video yet." I manage to get the words out of my mouth, which is going as dry as the desert.

"You have to check her out! Just check your messages; I'll send you a link to her video," Cole says.

"Thanks."

Before I have a chance to look, the rest of the boys, Ashley, and Julie come into the lobby. Ashley walks up and sits down on the other side of me. Her silence is unnatural, but I choose to let it go for the moment. A hotel lobby isn't the best place to get into anything. You never know who is waiting for an unflattering photo or story these days.

Once we are safely on our flight, I pull Ashley toward the back of the plane. Having her mad at me is one of the worst things that can happen to me these days. Once I know it's just the two of us in earshot, I take a deep breath.

"I'm really sorry; I was scared," I say.

"Carly, you're amazing. But c'mon! You could have talked to me." She looks at me with hurt-filled eyes.

"I'm really sorry." I breathe out. "How'd you know?" I ask.

"I think I've heard you sing a thousand times in the shower by now." She lets out a small laugh. "Plus, when I got back to our room, I found the mess of makeup you left all over the bathroom." She smiles at me.

"I'm sorry I didn't give you a heads-up, Ash." I pull her in for a hug.

"Yeah, it's OK. It's a great song," she tells me. "Deep breath. It's going to be OK."

"Thanks," I mumble into her shoulder. "What should I do?" I feel as if my airway is struggling to stay open.

"Breathe before you pass out!" Ashley quickly replies.

Taking a deep breath, I let Ashley guide me into one of the empty seats near us. My gaze locks on Scott's tablet a few rows in front of me, which is currently playing my uploaded video. I close my eyes as I focus on getting air into my lungs.

Ashley takes a seat beside me and patiently watches with a curious gaze. She appears thoughtful, which makes me wonder about her thoughts.

"So?" I say. "What should I do?"

"With your level of anxiety, I bet you're trying to figure out if you should delete the video, and of course, it's your choice. But if I were you, I'd take advantage of the opportunity being presented to you."

"Deleting the video does sound nice, but there are copies of it everywhere." I frown.

That's one thing I wasn't thinking of: the internet is forever. I can never post again, or I can keep going. My stomach churns at that idea, but Ashley is right about opportunities. Some people spend their whole lives trying, and here I am, famous overnight.

"You look like you've decided." Ashley laughs.

"Maybe it wouldn't hurt to keep going," I whisper to her. "I just need to work on worrying less about what my brother and everyone else think."

"It'll get better with time."

"Thank you for being supportive." I tentatively smile.

"I just wish I had been there to hold your hand as you uploaded the video," she murmurs.

"You were with me in thought, and that has to count for something," I reply.

"Now that you've decided, it's time you joined the world of social media," she says with a smile full of excitement.

"Oh boy, this sounds worrisome." I nervously chuckle.

We spend the rest of the plane ride downloading the different apps and creating accounts with a similar anonymous username. I tweak the profile's settings and then link it to my YouTube channel. It doesn't take long for the world to notice, because the follower counts across the accounts drastically increase. I look toward the front of the plane and see my brother snoring like a baby. A lump forms in my throat, and I quickly shove it down.

I want nothing more than to talk to him, but I know that would break our relationship. I decide to leave this secret as just that. I can't lose my brother.

When I hit a half million followers by the end of the day, reality hits me like a ton of bricks. This is becoming a big deal.

"What should be my first post?" I ask Ashley.

"You could thank them for their support or give them an update on when the next video will be out," she says.

"OK, that sounds like a good idea." I nod.

My first tweet is an announcement for my next video, which will be on Saturday. It's Thursday, so that leaves forty-eight hours to prepare. Now that I've committed myself to it, the pressure sets in. If I can't follow through on my words, nobody will believe me when it counts. There are thousands of messages flooding my notifications, which brings a smile to my face. I'm only able to reply to a handful before I'm forced to shut off my phone and tablet for our landing in South Carolina.

I slip my phone into my pocket and make my way off the plane with Ashley by my side. We quickly locate Julie on the tarmac to see where she needs us to go.

"It's raining," she says, "so we're having cars come around so we can avoid walking across the parking lots to the cars."

"OK." We both nod.

I take a seat on the pavement and return to replying to messages on Twitter and Instagram. I don't think I can ever get enough of this. I adore the support and heartwarming messages from people I've never met. Of course, there are negative comments too, but I try not to think about those. I slip my phone back into my purse as the cars come screeching to a stop near us.

Ashley, Julie, and I pile into one car, while the boys pile into another. We take off toward our hotel. When we stop at a red light, a nearby group of girls can be heard shrieking in excitement.

"I can't believe it!" one girl screams to her friends. "There are even a few celebrities acknowledging this girl. It looks like she's using the username @singerwithmakeup."

"I wish I could sing like that," another says.

"I wish she'd upload another video before Saturday or post something on her account. I'm addicted, and I need my next fix!" one of the girls says.

"For sure!" another shrieks.

"This is already surreal. Are you OK?" Ashley asks me, leaning over.

"Yes." I sigh. "As long as Aiden doesn't kill me when he finds out."

"It's not Aiden's business," she says a little too curtly.

I wonder where I've heard that before.

"Singerwithmakeup is one to watch," Ashley reads gleefully from an article on her phone. "Peppered with spice and cinnamon, her voice is delightfully seasoned, and it leaves us hungry for more."

I hold out a hand. "Oh, give me that."

"For all her sweet innocence"—Ashley continues, holding her phone out of my reach—"she has a pro's grip on her listeners."

"Ashley!" I succeed in wrestling her phone from her hands and stuff it triumphantly under one arm. "There," I say smugly. "No more reading reviews."

"Can we at least celebrate?" Ashley frowns.

"I suppose." I raise my eyebrows. "What do you have in mind?"

"I'll figure something out." Ashley gives me a sneaky smile. "I'll plan the party for after your post on Saturday." She grins.

<hr>

Saturday seems to fall into my lap, and I find my face caked in costume makeup and my hair teased over the opposite side of my face. I don't recognize myself. With a satisfied nod to myself, I sit down in front of my computer and pull my guitar onto my lap. It takes a few moments to tune the chords I'm searching for, but once I have them, I hit the button to record on the screen.

"Hi, everybody." I take a big, deep breath. "I first want to thank you for all your kind words of encouragement. It's important to me that my lyrics help those around me as they've helped me." I shift my guitar into position. "This song goes out to anyone who's still finding their way." I close my eyes and start in on the chords, letting the music flow through me.

Are you lost, or are you found?
Are both feet on the ground?
Only questions, no answers.
Floating along with your path of life.
Your choices will keep you in strife.

There's no question or shortage of pain.
You question and take God's name in vain.
You're here to be you each and every day.
The path you're on is your personalized way.

Face your demons; do it with grace.
For life is a dance and not a race.
Listen to the music playing Saturday nights.
Keep pushing; you'll find your path with lights.

There's no question or shortage of pain.
You question and take God's name in vain.
You're here to be you each and every day.
The path you're on is your personalized way.

I let the chords fade out before I look up at the camera and smile. "Thank you for listening. Remember, you're not alone. Until next time." I give a little wave before I click the button to stop recording.

Sitting back in my chair, I blow out a breath that I seem to have been holding. It only takes a few clicks with my mouse to tweak a few aspects of the video before I post it online. My phone pings with an incoming message from Ashley. I take that as my cue to shut my computer and clean myself up for the party.

I arrive downstairs, where I find the party is in full swing in the hotel ballroom. Ashley has outdone herself with this one. People are arriving by the dozens, sporting expensive designer dresses and suits. Outside the floor-to-ceiling windows, the moon acts as a natural disco ball, lighting the ballroom. Dainty fairy lights add color to the parade footsteps.

Greetings are exchanged between the guys in the band and those in attendance. A sweet, soft melody drifts through the busy atmosphere, coming from the ballroom. I catch hints of smells of lavender and orchids placed at various intervals around the room. I start weaving my way through the crowds of champagne-bearing waiters, keeping an eye out for Ashley.

Out of nowhere, I feel a slight tug on my elbow and look up into the glittering, amused eyes of Scott. I realize what he's looking for, and I let him smoothly lead me onto the dance floor. Our feet glide effortlessly across the pearlescent floor. I feel myself start to relax a bit into his arms as he slows down the dance.

"Ashley sure knows how to throw a party, doesn't she?" He leans down to whisper in my ear.

"She sure does." I smile up at him.

"Any idea why she wanted to throw such a glamourous party?

It's almost like a celebration of some sort." His eyes are practically boring into my soul.

I gulp. I want so badly to tell him what's been going on. "I have no idea," I tell him without meeting his eyes.

He gently lifts my chin so that I meet his eyes. "Yes, you do," he says with a knowing look.

I struggle to swallow the lump in my throat. Everybody and everything seemingly slow down and freeze around the two of us. I can still feel the low bass vibrating through my heels.

Unfortunately, Kyle and Cole choose this moment to appear with a tray of drinks and colorful shots of different liquors. They are oblivious to the tender moment between Scott and me.

"Well, I, for one, am excited," Kyle says, draping an arm around my shoulders. "I have no idea why Ashley wanted this party so bad, but I'm always up for a good time. What's your drink of choice, Carly?" He nods to the tray. "Rum and Coke? Dark and Stormy? Sweet and Sexy?"

"She doesn't—" Scott coughs.

"Vodka soda," I say, shooting Scott a look.

I will be damned if Scott tells the boys I stay away from hard liquor. It is kind of true since I prefer wine, but for one night, I feel like being somebody else. I feel like being a braver version of myself. To my surprise, Scott grins from ear to ear.

"You heard the lady," he tells Kyle. "Get her a drink."

I watch as Kyle disappears back to the bar.

"You've really never been one for alcohol," Scott says.

"Nope."

"What's changed all of a sudden?" He raises his eyebrows at me.

"Everything." I shrug. "And nothing."

"You're full of surprises, Carly." Scott shoots me a flirty wink.

It's not long before I start to feel the effects of the sweet drink Kyle has placed in my hand. Time seems to slow down for me as I start to feel a sense of numbness flow over my body. I look around and notice what's going on around me. Aiden and some gorgeous redhead are making out on one of the couches off to the side. Cole and Kyle are knee deep in flirting with a group of girls nearby with glasses of multicolored drinks. I practically bump into Scott as I turn around to look for Ashley.

"Sorry," I slur. "I'm trying to find Ashley." I stumble more into him.

"Come on," Scott says, guiding me by the waist over to a set of empty sofas to sit down. "You're going to drink some water."

"But I—"

"Not a question."

I see something in his eyes flash that causes something deep in my heart to stir.

"You're a lightweight." Scott scowls.

"Oh, that's rich." I snort, rolling my eyes. "You know, if I want an older brother trailing me around all night, I can go get Aiden."

Scott flinches. He starts shaking slightly. The lighting is dim, and we manage to sit off in an abandoned corner. The couch doesn't allow for much space between us. This means I can see his full expression. I can tell I hit a nerve.

"But I'm not," Scott says softly. "I'm not your brother, Carly."

My heartbeat kicks up into overdrive.

My mind flashes back to that day when Scott was sitting in my hotel room after I got out of the shower, horrified at the idea of seeing me naked. What did he say again? "Carlz, I practically raised you."

"But you said—" I swallow. "You told me you think of me like a sister."

"I lied."

"And you're with Alissa."

"Not anymore." Scott's green eyes go dark. "We broke up."

"You did? But why?" My mind is going a million miles a second.

Scott makes an exasperated noise. "Because I can't stop thinking about you."

And just like that, he tilts my chin up and kisses me.

I freeze. Scott's hands snake expertly around the back of my waist, cradling me firmly, but they are shaking slightly, as if he half expects me to push him away.

But I don't. I pull him closer.

Scott groans, slanting his head toward me. I can taste tequila and peppermint and something spicy on his tongue, something uniquely Scott, sending passionate shocks throughout my entire nervous system. His hands, calloused from years of guitar, slide under my tank top to touch the bare skin of my waist, and the sensation sends an electric jolt through me.

Floodlights light up the entire ballroom out of nowhere, causing the two of us to fling apart as if struck by lightning. I work to focus on what's going on, and I see Ashley. She's extremely intoxicated, and she has a microphone onstage.

The spotlight illuminates the stage, where Ashley is swaying slightly with an orange drink in one hand and the microphone in the other. Her dress is a glorious design of crystals and rose gold that makes her look like a shining star under the lights. A shining start that I suddenly get a bad feeling about.

"Scott," I say as I meet his eyes, "we need to get Ashley off that stage. Now." I feel panic rising in my chest.

Scott gazes over at his sister on the stage, and it's as if a lightbulb goes off in his head but for completely different reasons, I assume. It's as if time starts to fast-forward as we both jump up from the sofa and frantically move through the crowd toward the stage.

"I just want to thank everyone for coming to celebrate with us tonight!" Ashley says with intoxicated glee. "Carly appreciates it more than you all know!" She sways slightly, causing her drink to slosh a bit onto the floor.

Her statement makes my blood turn cold, causing me to freeze. Scott whips his head around, and we lock eyes. I can see everything click into place on his face.

"Cole! Kyle!" Scott barks at the two, who are standing closer to the stage, dumbstruck. "Get Ashley out of here—now!" he shouts at them.

Cole swallows and gives a nod in understanding.

"Carly, where are you out there?" Ashley slurs a bit into the microphone as she squints into the crowd through the spotlights. "I want us all to share in expressing how proud of you we are for sharing your music. Your online videos have been inspiring to so many listeners."

Her words bounce off the choking silence of the ballroom.

"C'mon, everyone! Let's give my favorite person in the world a round of applause for her bravery and success! Check out her latest video from today!" Ashley shouts with glee.

I watch, frozen with horror, as Cole and Kyle reach the stage and grab the drink and the microphone from Ashley. They hand the items off to someone random and shuffle Ashley off the stage, effectively removing her from the entire party out a side door.

The whole ballroom falls deathly silent. My ears start ringing with the inability to process what's happening. *There's no way this is happening*, I think.

I hear whispers and gasps as everyone around me starts to piece together Ashley's words. Everywhere I look, it feels as if someone is pointing a finger in my direction. I suddenly feel as if everything is moving in slow motion. The alcohol in my system is hindering my ability to fully process what's going on. I inevitably stumble and fall into a rock-hard chest. A feeling of safety washes over me as I recognize Scott's cologne. He wraps his arms around me protectively. The sound of glass shattering cuts through the building tension in the room.

"Tell me she's joking!" a pain-filled voice yells. The voice belongs to the one person I've feared telling this secret to the most: Aiden.

"Scott, I have to talk to Aiden. I have to explain." With white-hot tears running down my face, I try to wiggle out of the steel cage of his arms.

"Carly, stop. He's not going to hear anything you say tonight." His grip holds fast.

"No, he can. He has to!" I cry as I wiggle around so I'm facing away from him.

"Tonight's not the night. I need to get you out of here."

His words aren't making sense to me.

I cast my eyes around the room until I find Aiden. The sight of him causes me to shed more hot tears. More than a dozen glasses are shattered at Aiden's feet. Two security guards are holding Aiden and pleading with him to calm down. He's in a blind rage. I watch in horror as he throws one of the security guards to the side.

"Aiden! Stop! Please!" I cry out to him, begging.

I watch as he whips his head around and meets my eyes. I can see the betrayal plain as day on his face.

"Tell me it's not true! Tell me it's not you in those videos!" he yells at me.

My silence seems to provide him the answer he needs. With a final look of betrayal cast my way, he throws himself out the emergency exit a few feet behind him. I stand limply in Scott's arms with hot tears running down my face.

"Carly, I'm getting you out of here."

The nerves in his voice bring me back to my current predicament. That's when I notice the flashes from different cameras around me. I realize there are a few cell phones out, recording. I don't get a chance to put words together, though, before Scott lifts me swiftly off my feet and begins carrying me out of the ballroom bridal-style. When we step onto the elevator, pandemonium hits, and everyone starts trying to flood after us. With a tiny bit of luck, the door closes with a ding just in time.

Chapter 9

We arrive safely back at my hotel room. Scott sets me down in a chair as I finally start to digest the events that have just unfolded. For me, the world seems to be falling apart. My heart is filled with melancholy; my fists are continuously clenching in frustration and anger. Yet I do not cry. It's almost as if I physically can't cry. The shock of the betrayal hasn't worn off. My life, my family—nothing is going to be the same after tonight. I feel shattered beyond repair.

But then I look up, my eyes meet Scott's, and I feel the tiny pieces of myself that were just shattered start to twitch back together. That's when it dawns on me: he wasn't surprised at all by Ashley's announcement.

"You knew, didn't you?" I ask.

"I figured it out. Once I recognized your voice, everything else made sense." He kneels in front of me.

"You didn't say anything to Aiden. To me."

"It wasn't my place to say anything," he says with a slight shrug.

"I'm not sure how I'm going to dig myself out of this mess in the morning." I let out a frustrated sigh. "I can't believe Ashley." I tremble in anger. I press my fingers to my eyes to stop the tears that are starting to prick at them.

"She had no right to her actions tonight," Scott says with a steady tone to his voice.

"What am I supposed to do?" I ask him with a voice that's starting to crack. "Should I go find Aiden?"

"Definitely not. Let the dust settle tonight. Kyle found him and has him cooling off before coming back to the hotel for bed." He lifts a hand and uses his thumb to wipe a tear off my cheek. "The sun will rise in the morning just like it always does, Carly," he says gently.

I'm not sure if it's the lingering tension between us from the kiss downstairs or if my brain has truly short-circuited completely, but I lean in and capture his lips with mine. That seems to be the only hint Scott needs. The sexual tension between us passes the boiling point. He leans down and scoops me up bridal-style with his lips still locked on mine. Both of us hungrily try to taste every bit we can.

He lays me on my bed, tumbling down right after me. Gripping my hands in his, he dives into the kiss like a starving man. I feel myself giving in to his hot kisses, giving in to him, sliding far past the point of no return. Need washes over us like a low, constant vibration.

He runs his hands up my body and down my back, seemingly testing my shape and etching it into his memory. My body is completely under his control. He draws away and places a hand on my cheek; our heartbeats thud in rhythm.

"You're exquisite," he murmurs as he uses his mouth to start removing my top.

He tugs off my shirt, and I waste no time in returning the favor—more flesh, more muscle.

I run my hands over his chest, breathing out. "Mmm, yes."

I want to look at him, just look, but I can't stop his hands. When he works off my lacy bra and captures one of my breasts with his mouth, I lose all traces of coherent thought. My back arches, and he takes the opportunity to slip my skirt completely off.

"I should slow down," he says breathlessly, seemingly struggling for some sense of control or even a little finesse, as he eases back.

"No," I say, and I wiggle to help him strip me down. "No, you shouldn't."

"Thank God." He lets out a groan.

"Let me." I work my quick, capable hands between us, loosening his belt. "Let me." As I drag at his pants, I roll us over so he can kick free of them and then roll again, greedy to take.

Slow can wait. I want fast and fierce and free. Here with him, I want the loss of control for both of us. I want to steep in the mindless desperation of it all—to be touched, to be wanted, to feel the need pulsing in him just as it does in me.

When he plunges into me at last, the pleasure strikes sharp as an arrow.

My hips pump, and my fingers dig into his sides as I revel in the power and speed. Release rips through me, leaving me trembling, gasping, and grateful. And still, he drives me, building it all again. I'm forced to hold on, matching him beat for frantic beat. When I crash again, when my hands, which are gripping him, slide weakly away, he falls with me.

⸺◈⸺

I wake up and immediately panic. *Oh God.*

I just slept with the biggest pop star in the country. It's much more terrifying because it's Scott. I look around and notice he isn't around, so I can simply get dressed, go to the living room, and have breakfast as if everything is normal. Aiden is always an early riser, which means it won't be long before he—

I freeze. *Aiden.*

I flop back onto the bed, staring at the ceiling. I know my brother is going to kill me. After the events of last night, he's going to kill me and then Scott. They might be best friends, but if Aiden finds out we slept together, I'm certain he will chop Scott into tiny pieces and scatter him across the beach outside our hotel. I groan. Sleeping with Scott was a bad idea.

I feel panic swell in my chest. *This is bad.*

It's worse than the time Ashley and I got drunk on strawberry martinis and flashed a whole apartment building in Colorado. I groan. The events of the night before come back to me in waves. My disbelief in Ashley's actions almost has me paralyzed where I lie. With a shake of my head, I start to pull myself together. Cautiously, I scramble out of bed and search for clothes. I change into a pair of jeans and a blue tank top and yank on socks at random.

Then, before I can change my mind, I grab my phone and flee to the bathroom. Safely sequestered in the spacious marble room, I punch in a familiar number and hold the phone up to my ear. Sophia picks up on the first ring.

"Hello?"

"I've done something bad," I blurt out.

"Oh, good," Sophia says. "I've been waiting for this day."

I hear a door shut.

"Hit me with it," she says.

So I do.

I recount the night's events, starting with the kiss at the party and ending with waking up in an empty bed. I keep some of the details to myself—there is only so much I want to share, after all—but by the time I'm done, I'm out of breath.

"So?" I say. "What do you think?"

"I can't believe you and Scott finally climbed into bed together," Sophia says.

"What?"

"Seriously, it's about time," Sophia drawls, sounding amused. "First of all, I've seen you and Scott orbit each other for years. Trust me—this is a good thing."

"Sophia!" I hiss.

"And secondly," Sophia says, unperturbed, "he probably had to get up for a meeting or something. I'm sure it's not what it looks like."

I concede that is a valid point. "But what do I do?" I moan, sliding backward into the bathtub. "What do I say to Scott? I really like him, Soph."

"Oh no." Sophia's voice turns alarmed. "No, no. I don't do feelings, remember? You have Ashley for that."

"But I can't call Ashley!"

"Why not?"

"It's her brother." I cover my eyes with a hand. "And anyway, after last night—" I break off as my phone vibrates. "Oh, hang on. I'm getting a call."

"Ashley?"

"No." I frown. "It's an unknown number."

I let the call go straight to voice mail and fill Sophia in on the events that took place last night with Ashley's surprise drunken announcement. I lay it all out for her and even explain the secret and why I hid behind the makeup: to avoid the fact that my brother would hate me. But now he does. I explain to her that I'm not mad at Ashley but am hurt. Sophia helps to calm me down from a potential panic attack and swears to check in on Ashley and report back to me so I know how she's doing and how to proceed with that. What's done is done; it's time to hash things out and move forward. I've never been good with conflict of any sort.

After I hang up ten minutes later, I punch the button for my voice mail. *It's probably a telemarketer. Or one of those annoying automated messages. If I have to hear one more time about how I can benefit from life insurance, I—*

"Hi, Carly," a voice says. "This is Gabe from Tune City Records."

I almost drop my phone. I listen, slack-jawed, as Gabe proceeds to tell me he saw my video online the other night, received a tip that I'm the one in the video, and loves my work. He asks if I would be interested in coming to New York for a meeting at some point to discuss an EP.

I blank. Then I listen to the message again.

Holy shit. This is real. This is happening.

My whole body is shaking. I walk to the sink and press a damp towel to my flushed face. A helium balloon is expanding in my chest, slamming in time with my heartbeat. Gabe Palman from Tune City Records wants to meet with me.

Everyone knows Gabe. He represents Scarlett. He represents the new country star who just won *American Idol*. Hell, Gabe represents half the music industry.

And he wants to represent me.

I set down the towel, breathing hard. I need to call Ashley. *She'll know what to do.*

Even after the events of last night, she's still my best friend. I can't stay mad at her.

Oh, to hell with it. I'll tell her about Scott too. I grin as I reach for my phone and scroll through my contacts.

The door clicks open.

Abruptly, I bound into the room.

"Scott!" I shut the bathroom door behind me. "I need to tell you something. I—"

"Me first," he says.

I pause. I watch, frowning, as Scott carefully sets a plate of croissants and melon on the table. His mouth is set in a grim line.

"Carly," he says, "I'm so sorry."

My heart takes a nosedive off a cliff. I sink onto the bed, trying not to assume the worst. But I know Scott. And I know that look.

"Sorry for what?" I ask.

Scott runs a hand through his mop of dark curls. "Look, I wasn't in my right mind last night. And I don't think you were either."

I feel the words like an icy slap. I was slightly drunk and emotional last night, but I still wanted Scott. I have always wanted him. Drinking didn't change that.

"What are you trying to say?" I ask. My mouth is dry, and my body is numb.

"Do you want a croissant? I brought croissants." Scott turns away.

I can see the muscles in his back rippling as he pulls on his shirt. "Scott?"

"Or coffee," he adds. "Most of yours spilled, but there's still—"

"Scott." My heart is rocketing. "Look at me, please."

Slowly, he turns. There is so much guilt in his expression that I feel the balloon in my chest pop and deflate into scraps of rubber.

Oh no. I'm an idiot.

For a second, I thought I might have been different. Different from all the other girls. But now, looking at his face, I know the truth.

"We made a mistake," Scott says, drilling a hole in my heart deeper.

"A mistake?"

"I didn't—" He shakes his head. "I mean, you're Aiden's younger sister, Carly. You're off-limits. I shouldn't have gone there."

"You shouldn't have kissed me then," I say coolly, and Scott flinches. I cross my arms. I feel my eyes stinging, but I will be damned if I cry in front of Scott Harris. I refuse to.

"I know."

"And you shouldn't have stayed after getting me back to my room."

"Technically," he says, "you didn't tell me to leave, though."

I suck in a sharp breath. His words hurt because they're true. I should have known better. Haven't I seen Scott go through girls like tissues over the years? Don't I know how convincing he is? How stupidly charming he can be when he wants to be? Sure, Scott told me last night that he likes me, but what does that matter? He probably says that to every girl to get her into bed. And I was stupid enough to fall for it.

My stomach rolls. "So what?" I arch an eyebrow. "You want to just forget about it?"

"I don't want—" Scott perches awkwardly against the dresser with his long legs stretched out in front of him. "Look, can we just keep this to ourselves? At least for now?"

My insides clench. *Translation: Don't tell Aiden.*

I want to cry and to scream. I want to grab all the pillows on the bed and throw them at him one by one and maybe the TV remote too. That's what Sophia would have done. But I'm not like that.

And I'm not about to let Scott know he's hurt me.

"Fine," I say.

"Fine?" Scott blinks.

"We'll forget about it." I shrug.

Scott's expression flickers for a moment, as if I've hit a nerve, but then he nods and begins to pull on his shoes.

"Thanks," he says gruffly.

And that's that.

I'm not sure how I manage it, but I make small talk as he gathers his things, nibbling on some fruit for breakfast. I don't think my stomach can take anything heavy or greasy. When he finally leaves, I fall back onto my bed, staring up at the ceiling.

Well, shit.

My heart feels as if it's tearing itself in half. After a decade of loving Scott, this is what things have come down to: rejection.

I desperately wish to call Ashley. But that potentially would make things worse. I simply need to learn to live with it. I sit up, force myself to drink some juice and brush my teeth, and then force myself to walk down to the lobby. I smile at the concierge as I pass and step out into the blazing sunshine.

This is fine. I'm fine.

I wander to a nearby park and sit cross-legged on a bench beneath a cedar and a wrought-iron lamppost. Once I'm sure my breathing is under control, I press the redial button.

Gabe picks up on the third ring.

"You've got Palman."

"Hi, Mr. Palman." I grip my phone tightly; my hands are slick with nerves. "This is Carly Taylor."

"Carly!" Gabe's voice perks up. "I'm so glad you returned my call."

I hear a shuffle of papers and then the closing of a door.

"You got my message then?" he says.

"I did," I say. "And I'm interested in meeting. What day works for you?"

We compare schedules, settling on next Monday early in the afternoon. Gabe promises to send a car to the airport to collect me, although I draw the line at his paying for a first-class plane ticket to New York. I refuse to feel as if I owe him anything, just in case.

I hang up the call, and it dawns on me: *I'm really doing this. I'm meeting with Gabe Palman.*

My nerves kick into overdrive. For a brief second, I wish Scott would come with me. Or even Aiden. They both have experience in the music industry and would know if Gabe pulls anything shady. But after last night, I think I'd rather snap my precious guitar in half than ask either of them to come to New York with me. Besides, I feel a sinking rock forming in the pit of my stomach, as I fear that Aiden isn't going to take the news of my EP well.

I come out of my thoughts and look around the plaza. I see many carefree and spirited teenagers milling around. Some are laughing, some are listening to music, and others are seemingly working on coursework with textbooks and laptops. I chew on my bottom lip. I can always ask Cole, I suppose, but he would feel honor-bound to tell the boys, which defeats the purpose.

That leaves only one option.

I pick up my phone again and punch in a number. He picks up immediately.

"Hey, pretty girl." He immediately puts a smile on my face.

"Kyle." I squeeze my eyes shut. "I have a favor to ask of you. A big one." I screw up my courage, taking a deep breath. "How would you feel about coming to New York with me next Monday?"

Chapter 10

G abe Palman's office looks more like a greenhouse than the typical professional office. Every surface in the room is made of glass: the desk, the paperweights, and a ladder that holds a variety of potted green plants. Even the far wall is made of glass, offering a sweeping view of Times Square's glittering lights and crowds of people. Not that I can see a lot with Gabe pacing back and forth in front of it.

"Coffee?" he says. "Tea? Water?"

"No, thank you," I say. I glance over at Kyle, who shakes his head too.

"Right." Gabe stops pacing. "Let's get down to business then." He takes a seat at his desk, placing his hands in a steeple. "I want ten tracks. Original music. The same style you posted online."

Despite the fact that I'm sitting beside Kyle, the drummer for one of the most famous bands in the world, Gabe's gaze doesn't waver from my face. It dawns on me that he's serious about me, not just for my connection to Shade.

"What are you offering?" I ask after a moment.

"A record deal," Gabe says nonchalantly. "And I'll give you thirteen percent in royalties."

"You might as well pay her in pennies!" Kyle scoffs.

"Why are you here again?" Slowly, Gabe shifts his gaze to Kyle, looking at him as if he's a slimy slug that just rolled into his office.

"Consider me her agent." Kyle's smile is firm and cool.

"You want a cut?"

"No," Kyle says pleasantly. "I'm just here to make sure you don't screw her over." He picks up a paperweight and fiddles with it idly. "Twenty percent."

Gabe's eyes narrow. "Fifteen percent."

"Eighteen," Kyle says coldly. "And she gets to keep her rights after a year." He begins to play hot potato with the paperweight. "That's a damn good offer, considering her recording sales will be off the charts."

"I want exclusivity on the EP," Gabe says as he straightens in his chair.

Kyle scowls. "That's not—"

"That's fine." I cut in. "But that means you're signing my album. Not me." I smile at him sweetly. "And Kyle's right. I want twenty percent."

Kyle shifts to look at me in surprise, and my lips twitch. I might have brought him to New York as backup, but I'm not totally incompetent in the world of music. My parents own a studio, after all, and I have Aiden as an older brother.

"You drive a hard bargain, Carly Taylor." Gabe smiles.

"I know what I'm worth," I say simply.

"Fair enough." Gabe shrugs. "Twenty percent, and you keep your rights to the EP. But I get the option to buy your next album first."

We finish haggling out the details, and then I sign a mountain of paperwork; my hand cramps up as I tear through the forms. Kyle looks over each document I sign, but he doesn't say anything, not until we leave the building, stepping out into the buzzing of crowds and New York humidity.

"Well, well," Kyle says, grinning. "All of those business classes paid off." He swings an arm over my shoulders. "You're a shark, Carly Taylor."

"Oh, shut up." I snort.

"Seriously. You didn't need me in there."

"Maybe not," I say, "but I wanted you there."

There's a long, drawn-out pause, and I start to blush crimson.

Oh shit. That came out wrong.

I'm about to blurt out what would undoubtedly be an embarrassing, rambling explanation, when Kyle grins.

"You know what we need?" he asks.

"A stiff drink?"

"A slice of pizza," he says, steering me through the crowd. "We have just enough time to grab some airport pizza before our flight back."

I know something is wrong as soon as we return to South Carolina.

Julie is waiting for us in the hotel lobby, tapping her foot impatiently. She is dressed in a black suit, her frizzy brown hair is slicked into a chignon, and she is wearing professional pink lipstick.

My heart sinks.

"Oh no," Kyle mutters.

Julie's eyes catch on mine, and she makes a beeline for us, almost knocking over a terrified bellboy carrying a large stack of suitcases.

"Where the hell were you?" she snarls.

"We went on a dolphin cruise." I glance at Kyle.

We are both dressed in business-casual clothing. Hell, I'm still in black heels. Thankfully, Julie is too riled up to notice

"And you couldn't pick up your phones?" Julie says.

"We didn't have reception," I say. "Why?"

"Care to explain this?"

Julie slaps a glossy magazine into my hand. For a terrifying moment, I think the news about the EP somehow got leaked, but then I glance down, and my stomach plunges and splats on the ground.

Oh no.

The cover is a blurry shot of Scott and me getting into the elevator together after the fiasco at the party at the hotel. I'm bundled in Scott's leather jacket, with my blonde hair spilling down the back of it. Scott is carrying me bridal-style. The headline reads, "Scott's Secret Heartbreak."

The irony cuts like a knife.

"Oh God." I suck in a breath. "Has Aiden seen it?"

"Not yet." Julie's mouth is a thin line.

"But it's just a shot of them going into the elevator, right? Isn't that a bit of a stretch?" Kyle frowns, peering over my shoulder.

"After the party events," Julie says pointedly. "And with her in his arms." She snatches the magazine back. "It doesn't help that your top is so low cut. The optics aren't great."

"That's not fair." My temper flares.

"You should know better."

"Scott should know better," I snap. "Seriously, Julie?" I cross my arms over my chest. "Are you really shaming me for wearing a low-cut top right now?"

"That's not what I—" Julie deflates slightly.

"Yes, it is." I interrupt her, setting my chin. "That's exactly what you're doing."

Julie mumbles an apology. Even though I'm slightly mortified, I nod in acceptance. My heart is racing. In all honesty, I don't have much of a leg to stand on. Julie might be wrong about my top, but she is right that I should have known better. Of course there were paparazzi at the party. What if one of them had seen the pair of us kissing?

Oh God. What if my parents have seen the tabloid?

My head starts to spin.

"I need to talk to Aiden," I say. "Especially if he hasn't seen the tabloid yet. Do you know where he is?"

"He's out."

"Oh." I deflate. "Where?"

"He's taping an interview," Julie says grimly. "With Scott. Downtown."

"Then take me there," I tell her, not asking. "I need to be the one to tell him about this magazine cover."

<hr>

I resist the urge to press my face up to the glass. Below, Scott and Aiden are seated on a black leather couch. Clyde Simmons, the late-night show host, sits at a desk beside them. Even from the lighting booth, I can see that Clyde is caked in at least three layers of foundation. He looks redder in person, more tomato-like.

I give myself a mental shake. *Focus.*

He is currently asking the boys which drinks they keep on their tour bus, and the audience is in stitches as Scott describes their ongoing battle to claim the last Coke Zero. His green eyes glow under the stage lights.

My heart twists painfully. He is unfairly attractive. Even now, after he broke my heart.

Next to me, Julie shifts. "They should be done soon." She checks her watch. "Five more minutes."

I nod impatiently.

I'm vaguely aware of Clyde swiveling in his chair, and then a large projector screen unfolds behind him. My insides clench. Next to me, Julie stiffens.

"What the hell?" she murmurs. "This wasn't in the prep notes."

Clyde clicks a button, and my heart stops working.

On the screen is a blown-up version of the tabloid I held myself. Clyde says something, gesturing toward the image with his hands. Aiden's face is white. Scott, on the other hand, is completely expressionless. But his hands are twisting in his lap.

"Oh no," I whisper. "No, no."

"So I have to ask," Clyde says, oblivious to my inner meltdown. "What exactly is the deal with you and Carly Taylor, Scott?"

To my surprise, Scott grins easily. "Oh, come on, Clyde." He waggles a finger. "You should know not to trust tabloids."

The audience laughs.

Clyde is undeterred. "You're denying it then?"

"Of course he is," Aiden says, jumping in. "It's ridiculous. That's my little sister."

"Scott?" Clyde says patiently.

Scott shifts on the leather couch. The studio audience has gone eerily quiet, and I can hear my own heartbeat hammering in my ears. Next to me, Julie is mouthing silent words. I'm pretty sure she is praying for a swift end to the interview.

Scott shrugs. "I've known Carly forever," he says.

"And you're not dating her?" Clyde says.

"No."

"So the rumors aren't true?" Clyde asks shrewdly. "There's nothing romantic going on between the two of you?"

"No," Scott says firmly. "She's like a sister to me."

I freeze. I'm dimly aware of Clyde steering the conversation back to safer waters and of the audience laughing at something Aiden says, but it all feels far away from me. I can only concentrate on Scott's painfully calm expression. He looks fine. Totally and completely fine.

I thought my heart was already broken, but it seems to splinter further somehow, cracking into trillions of little pieces. Scott just admitted on live television that he thinks of me as a sister. It doesn't get any clearer than that.

Next to me, Julie breathes a sigh of relief. "Thank God," she murmurs. "He nipped that in the bud, eh?"

I swallow the lump in my throat. "I have to go. I'll find my way back to the hotel."

I walk out into the streets of the city with my head spinning from Scott's words. I feel used, ashamed, and stupid even. I stop outside a coffee shop and fall into one of the patio chairs. I don't shed any tears; I stubbornly tell myself he's not worth it. But my brother and best friend are worth it. I allow myself a few minutes to gather my thoughts and formulate a plan—a plan to fix things with my brother and stop being mad at and avoiding Ashley. With my intentions set, I hail a cab and rattle off the address to the driver.

With traffic, it takes about half an hour for the driver to weave in and out of cars like a magician. A few cars honk in our direction, but the driver seems to pay no attention to them. He swiftly pulls up to the front of the hotel, and I pass him some green bills and say thanks for the ride. I notice some paparazzi chilling off to the side of the building, which clues me in that Aiden isn't back yet from the interview. That means Ashley defaults to first in my plan.

I sneak into the building quickly without alerting attention to myself and head straight for the elevator. I breathe in and out a few times to steady myself as I press the button for the top floor, where all our rooms are. I know from talking with Kyle that Ashley is crashing in Julie's room. According to a GPS sharing app she and I use to share our active locations with each other, she should be currently in. I knock a few times on the door and wait anxiously for her to answer.

"Can we talk?" I ask Ashley when she answers the door.

"Yes, please," she says with a look of relief on her face. She lets me in and shuts the door behind me.

We find spots opposite each other on the sofa.

"I think it's safe to say we've all had our fair share of shitty drunken mistakes," she says.

I nod in recognition.

"I'm really, truly one thousand percent sorry, Carly. I really don't know what came over me at the party," Ashley says with tears in her eyes.

"I definitely felt betrayed and still do a bit," I tell her gently. "Because we're best friends. You're practically my sister, and you spilled the biggest secret."

"I know. All I can remember is feeling so damn proud of you when I saw some people watching the video you had posted that night. Then the next thing I remember is being pulled offstage and escorted to Julie's room. Then it all goes black. I found some video footage online, though. Which is extremely embarrassing."

"Yes, the footage online didn't waste any time—that's for sure," I say as I rub my hands over my face. "But what's done is done. I hate being mad at you." I toss a couch pillow at her for emphasis.

"I hate you being mad at me." She grins at me as she catches the pillow.

"I've got some time before Aiden gets back. I have some news to share with you before I go corner him." I keep the dread out of my voice.

"Yeah, sorry about that one." She hangs her head again. "Let me know if I can help fix that."

I scoot over to sit next to her and pull her into a bone-crushing hug. "It's something I need to handle myself," I tell her. "There is something I will need your absolute support in as my best friend, though: my album that's been signed with an EP." I spill out the exciting news to her.

"Are you serious?" she asks me with eyes the size of globes.

"As serious as I was when I told you I wasn't wearing heels to our senior prom." I chuckle a bit at the memory.

"This is the best news ever!" she shrieks.

We spend the next hour or so going over all the details I know so far about the album, and she double pinkie promises not to go blabbing to the press with the news. I leave Julie's room, feeling refreshed.

However, the feeling quickly fades as I see Aiden entering his room down the hall.

Chapter 11

Seeing Aiden go into his room, I immediately feel the urge to run and hide somewhere like a recluse. Instead, I hold my head up high and push myself down the hallway toward his door. I stop myself just before knocking and give myself a pep talk. It's crazy, but I'm more nervous about facing my brother than I am about performing my songs. We've always been close, and I always have known that music would be a bone of contention between us. Before I get the chance to knock, the door is thrown open to reveal an irritated Aiden.

"What the hell are you doing outside my door?" he says, standing in the doorway with his arms crossed.

I cross my arms in response. "We need to talk," I tell him sternly.

He drops his hands to his pockets. "Seriously? You look like Mom when you stand like that."

I refuse to let my lips twitch into a smile.

He lets out a breath. "Shit. All right, come in." He gestures for me to follow him inside.

"Thanks." My voice stays flat. I close the door behind me softly, checking my attitude in the hallway. I remind myself I'm here to make amends, not continue to fight.

"Well, how are you?" Aiden awkwardly asks as he takes a seat on a barstool.

"Do you care?" I ask sharply. So much for my attitude staying checked in the hallway. "Because the last time I checked, you were ignoring me. Or ordering me around. Both sometimes."

Aiden winces. "Carly—"

"Do you deny it?" I cross the room and pull myself up onto the barstool next to him.

Aiden rests his head on his arms and doesn't say anything for a few minutes. The silence between us creates a void. He doesn't make eye contact, but he does sit back up after a couple of minutes, looking a little more relaxed.

"No," he says. "I have been ignoring you." He lets out a breath he seems to have been holding. "How long have you been composing?"

My whole life.

"Not long." I swallow the lump in my throat. "I picked it up more seriously in the last few months of college."

"You're pretty damn good for it not being all that long." Finally, Aiden meets my gaze.

I flinch. *Well, shit.*

"OK, so it's not just a hobby," I say, backtracking. "But I didn't think it would come to anything."

"Do Mom and Dad know?" Aiden asks.

"They know what you know now," I answer, being a tad cryptic. "Obviously, I had to loop them in after the party announcement."

"But Ashley's been in the loop?" Aiden says. "And Scott?"

"Scott worked it out on his own," I say finally.

"You know," Aiden says as his eyes narrow, "you never told me what he was doing in your room that night of the party."

"He wasn't doing anything, Aiden." I flush. I figure a little white lie will serve well here.

"Good," he says, looking relieved. "Because he's dating Alissa." He pauses. "And even if he wasn't, he wouldn't be allowed to date you."

"According to whom?" My eyes narrow into dangerous slits.

"According to me," he says simply. "You're my little sister, and Scott is my best friend."

I decide to let that go for now. "Let's back up. Tell me why you've been ignoring me."

His shoulders stiffen. "Can't we just drop it?"

Rage sticks to my ribs like hot wax. I feel my hands trembling. *Drop it. He wants to drop it.*

I put up with years of economics classes at university to make everyone happy because our parents wouldn't approve of a music degree. I stopped my guitar lessons when paparazzi showed up outside the studio. I did it all to protect Aiden, my famous older brother. And he wants to just leave it alone?

Well, I'm not having it anymore.

I climb down off the stool; cross to the couch; and seize a large, expensive decorative pillow. Then I hurl it at him, connecting with his left shoulder.

"Ow!" he yelps, twisting to face me. "What the hell?"

"I'm your sister!" I grab another pillow and hurl that one at him as well.

"Stop that!"

"Your only sister!" I hurl another smaller pillow missile. "You knew how much this all meant to me. Why the hell can't you be more supportive?"

"Calm down, Carly." Aiden dodges to the right.

"And when Ashley spilled the beans on my secret with the online videos, your first instinct that night was to accuse me! As if I've actually done something wrong!" I yell.

I hurl another pillow, narrowly missing his head.

Aiden stares at me as if I've sprouted a second head and a scaly tail. "Carly," he says, "stop throwing pillows at me. Fine. Let's talk calmly." He falls onto the now empty couch defeatedly.

"I've given up everything for you." My throat is raw. "Everything. My dreams, my life, my ambition, and even my love life. I have always been second best to you. Can't you be happy for me? Just this one time?"

"You don't mean that." Aiden goes white.

"But I do." I pace back and forth.

"I offered to pay for your university. I brought you on tour. I gave you things," he says, sounding confused. He truly doesn't understand.

I stop pacing and fall onto the couch next to him. "I never wanted those things," I whisper. "I never wanted your money." I squeeze a pillow from the floor to my chest. "I only wanted you, Aiden. I only wanted my brother."

"Carly," he manages to choke out through his own tears.

"No." I hold up a hand. "Just stop, Aiden. I don't want you to feel obligated to be my brother. I want you to want to be my brother." I break off, swallowing hard.

"I never meant to make you feel second best."

"You did. So did Mom and Dad," I choke out.

"Ah hell. Carly, I'm sorry." Aiden runs his hands through his hair. "I'll get on my hands and knees and beg if you need me to," he says as he kneels down in front of me.

"Don't be ridiculous." I shove his shoulder.

"I'm serious. I don't even know where to start with the apologizing. All I know is that you have always been the smarter, more talented, and more likable sibling. I've only had music. You've always had so much more," he says sincerely.

I wrap my arms around his neck, bringing him close for a tight hug. He hugs me back just as tightly. For the first time in a long time, I feel I understand where we are both coming from. This talk has been building for years, even without the help of the videos and the secret identity. I'm just glad we're hugging it out and not yelling and storming out. This is much more productive.

"What do we do now?" I ask after we pull away from our hug.

"I suppose that's up to you." He scratches his head.

"What do you mean?" I wrinkle my eyebrows in confusion.

"I mean you don't have to stay on tour with me if you don't want to. I'll help you go wherever you want to go to work on your album." He says the last part with a genuine smile.

It never occurred to me that I don't have to stay on tour with him and the guys. "Maybe I'll stick around awhile longer." I say it as if it's a question.

"Of course you can, Sis." He pulls me into a true brotherly hug. "You can hang around and tag along as long as you want."

We stay like that until Aiden's stomach growls, and we decide to go find dinner.

<hr />

I spend the next two weeks composing. The current leg of the tour is in Texas and is also the last. I opt to spend every hour I'm free out in a park somewhere with my guitar, scribbling down lyrics. Today, though, the downpouring rain has caused me to stay in the hotel. I wander toward the bathroom and look at myself in the mirror.

"You can do this," I whisper. "Only one more song to go."

After grabbing my guitar from the closet, I make myself comfortable in the living area, on the couch. I strum a few chords, tuning the strings and adjusting my wrist. I look around and say a silent thank-you prayer that the guys are all at a rehearsal.

> Just looking in your eyes
> takes me back to our goodbye.
> The movin' on comes in waves.
> The memory of us slowly fades.

I sing.

I end the verse on a soft note, allowing for a smooth transition into the second verse, which has an upbeat undertone.

> A bruised heart will never be the same.
> Both of us are to blame.
> You don't see the way you cut me up.
> I'm no longer part of your fan club.
> Now that I'm gone, you'll see
> just how much you'll miss me.

When I end the song, I look around for anybody. I smile into the responsive silence. Writing music has always been something incredibly personal to me.

I set my guitar to the side and lie down on the couch. It's hard to believe that just two weeks ago, I agreed to have ten songs ready to record, and I have done just that: I've created ten raw songs. I plan to throw everything I have into this album. I plan to start living my own life unapologetically for myself.

I check the time on my phone. I'm supposed to take Ashley to the airport in a few minutes. I painfully wish she didn't have to fly back to university to straighten things out. Interestingly, though, she now plans to take a year off after everything to figure out what she truly wants to do. The timing should work out for her to meet up with me in New York once she has everything squared away.

I grab my purse on the way out the door and head for the lobby to meet up with her and the driver Julie has scheduled.

After Ashley and I belt out a few songs at the top of our lungs later in the car, I find myself hugging her for dear life near the departure gate.

"You'll be fine," Ashley tells me, popping a strawberry into her mouth. "Just tell me if you hook up with someone, all right?"

"Ash!" I choke.

"What?"

"Stop it," I grumble, but I'm blushing, I never have gotten around to telling her about her brother. "Call me every day," I say, pulling her into one last fierce hug. "And don't forget to actually eat. Noodles aren't a real meal."

"Yes, ma'am." Ashley rolls her eyes.

"And give your poor liver a break sometimes."

"Duly noted."

We both laugh.

Finally, I let go of her. I wait until she disappears through security before making my way back out to the car.

It's not long before I arrive back at the hotel and run into the guys on their way out for a dinner event. Only Scott seems to notice my solemn silence, which is annoying.

"You're awfully quiet," he says, sipping on his water bottle.

"Everything OK?" He pushes his sunglasses back up onto his head. "Did Ashley get off OK?"

"She did, and I'm fantastic," I reply blandly.

"You're not upset?"

"Nope."

Scott's eyes feel as if they are penetrating my soul. There is a long, terrible pause.

"I've noticed you and Kyle are comfortable around each other," he says casually. "I saw him leaving your and Ashley's room last night. Anything going on there?"

I see red and almost throw my own water in his face. Kyle visited my room after the concert last night to listen to one of my new songs. We worked on it together until almost three in the morning. I didn't think anyone noticed, particularly Scott.

"It's none of your business, big brother," I say as icily as I can. I get brief satisfaction from seeing him slightly flinch. "But for your information, we're just friends," I add, dripping ice in my words.

"I doubt Kyle wants to be just friends," Scott says as he adjusts his sunglasses over his eyes. "I've seen the way he looks at you. He's just biding his time."

"That's a horrible thing to say." I glare at him.

"Maybe," he says, shrugging. "But it's also the truth."

I still haven't brought up what happened between us the night of the party, what happened after, or what Scott said in the interview, and I don't plan on it.

"If you'll excuse me"—I shuffle and sidestep around him—"I'm going to take a shower." I do everything in my power not to sprint up to my room.

He's wrong anyway. Kyle has been nothing but a good friend to me recently. He has listened patiently to rough verses and terrible choruses, and he has offered constructive criticism when I've asked for it.

I'm just finishing getting dressed, when I hear a knock on my door. I open it to see Kyle standing there with pancakes and coffee. I genuinely smile. It seems Kyle's been putting a smile on my face for a while now.

"This is what you got at brunch that one time, right?" Kyle asks unsurely.

"Yes." I blink.

"Good." He grins. "I got you a vanilla coffee too."

We head to the small table in my room and sit down.

"So what are you up to today before the concert? It is the last night of the tour," I say, stabbing at a few bites of pancake.

"We have a press event," he says with a slight grumble. "What are you going to be up to?"

"Well, I sent all ten sets of lyrics to Gabe and his team to review, so I think I'll just sightsee," I say as I wash down the pancakes with the coffee.

"Dang, girl! You're killing it," he says with a beaming smile.

Kyle takes off not long after I finish my coffee, so I head out exploring. Exploring by myself isn't bad. I wander through the heart of Dallas, admiring the sleek art deco buildings. I tour some of the historical museums, and by the time I return to the streets in search of a good barbecue sandwich, I'm feeling good. Great, actually. Better than I have in days.

Until I round a corner and run smack into a magazine stand. One magazine in particular catches my eye. The cover is a close-up shot of Scott and Alissa snuggled in a booth together, sharing what looks like a plate of fries. Scott is wearing a baseball cap low over his eyes, but there is no mistaking his white San Antonio Missions T-shirt. He purchased it only last week. My heart stops beating. The headline reads, "Scott Reignites an Old Flame." As if on cue, my cell phone rings.

"Hi, Ash," I answer, feeling numb.

"Carly." Ashley sounds breathless. "Are you with Scott? He won't answer his phone."

"He's at a press event," I tell her.

Ashley swears like a sailor, running through a list of creative expletives I have never once thought to string together.

"I'm going to kill him," Ashley growls. "Have you seen the papers?"

"I'm looking at them now."

"She's terrible!" Ashley yells. "I can't believe they're back together."

My whole body feels numb, and my chest feels as if a thousand-pound weight is crushing it. I think the image of Scott and Alissa has been stamped on the back of my eyelids like a permanent tattoo.

"Look, I've got to go," Ashley says. "But tell Scott to call me, OK?"

I hear the clink of a bottle opener. "I will."

"Good." Ashley pauses. "Is everything OK? You sound weird."

I grip my phone tightly. I desperately want to tell Ashley about Scott. I can't remember ever keeping a secret from Ashley, let alone one this big, and it is eating me up inside. But I can't do it. I don't want Ashley to think less of her brother, even if he and I hooked up and now ignore it.

"I do have some news," I say, thinking of the EP release date.

"But it can wait." I switch my phone to my other ear. "Remember to drink water tonight too, OK?"

"Yes, Mom."

"Love you."

"I love you more," Ashley coos, and then she hangs up the phone.

By the time I make my way back to the hotel, I have managed to calm myself down. So what if Scott and Alissa are back together? He doesn't owe me anything, and if he has bad taste in women, well, that isn't my fault. I race upstairs to get ready for this last concert. I wiggle into a fun fuchsia dress that stops at my knees. I pair my gold sandals with it and quickly touch up my makeup.

I check the time and see I only have a few minutes to meet Julie in the lobby. I practically sprint out of the room and down the hall to the elevator. I step off and immediately look around for Julie. I see her near the lobby doors, talking with Scott.

Great.

I desperately try to be invisible until Scott heads to the limousine. That quickly changes when I suddenly feel myself being thrown forward by a heavy force. I feel my head smack against the marble-tile floor. I feel something warm trickling down my cheek, and I sit up, feeling woozy.

"Carly!" Scott's panicked face appears in my vision. "Are you all right?" He cups my face. "Don't sit up. That'll make things worse."

"What are you—" I break off, slowly collecting my thoughts. "What just happened?"

"A bellboy just ran over you with a full luggage cart." He produces a tissue and dabs gently at my forehead, showing me the red blood. "Don't worry. I think Julie is going to have that kid's job."

He gestures to where Julie is now losing her temper on the kid and the hotel manager.

I start to sit up, but Scott holds me still.

"I've got it." I swat at his hand.

"You don't."

"I do," I snap, trying harder to stand up on my own.

"Carly, I swear. Just hold on a moment. There's a medical staff member coming over now."

I glare at him. "Seriously, Scott, I'm not broken," I say exasperatedly.

"Your skin is." He tilts my chin left and then right, examining the cut. "You bloody stubborn woman."

"Shut up, Scott," I snap. "Just because you're—" I don't get to finish my remark before I hear Aiden running across the hotel lobby with Cole and Kyle right behind him.

"What the hell happened?" Aiden asks everyone standing around.

"It's not as bad as it looks." I struggle to sit up.

"It's exactly that bad," Scott says.

"I feel fine," I say, feeling a little nauseous.

"Well," Aiden says, turning green as he takes in the blood, "that makes one of us. But seriously, what happened?" he asks Scott.

"That bellboy ran her over with a full luggage cart." Scott points in the direction of the kid, the hotel manager, and Julie, who is still going full on mama bear on them.

"Fantastic," Aiden says as he looks on at the situation.

"You got her? I have words to express as well." Without waiting for an answer from Aiden, Scott starts walking over to give Julie backup.

After I submit to being fussed over by what seems like every staff member in the hotel, plus Julie and the guys, it's finally determined that I don't have a concussion and that I'll be OK. I can't help but notice how quiet Scott and Kyle are both being.

Cole, on the other hand, has decided that bringing me chocolate while cracking jokes is his place in all of this. He does bring a few smiles to my face. As he is deep into a joke I've lost track of, I let Cole lead the way to one of the waiting cars outside. He finishes his joke as he opens the door for me.

"That's a good one." I smile at him as I climb in.

"Carlz, I started rambling. There was no joke." He winks at me. "But I figured it was better than awkward silence." He shrugs.

"Sorry, Cole. I appreciate it." I look up at him from inside the car.

"Don't mention it. Always here for you." He sticks a hand out to give me knuckles.

I giggle and bump my knuckles against his. He closes the door, and all the cars start to pull out. To the last concert we go.

The guys pull off the concert without any issues and drive the crowd nuts by stripping off their shirts and playing the last song shirtless. The stadium is so full of screaming girls that I can barely hear the music. I feel a sense of pride fill me as I watch my brother strum the last of the chords on his guitar. He's come a long way from just playing around in his room.

There's a sense of sadness as we all prepare to leave the stadium. I know the guys are all heading back to their families for some serious rest; this tour has been grueling on them all. Even though we are all going to be in Colorado—even Kyle, who now owns an apartment near the others guys—I know it's going to be different not to be around them all every day.

As the last of us buckle our seat belts and the plane takes off, I can't help but think that even though this adventure is ending, I have another one that's just beginning.

Chapter 12

When I stop stressing about life, it gets moving without my even realizing it, like a hazed blur. It seems as if it was just yesterday that I uploaded my first video. It's been a couple of months since that momentous occasion. Just over five million people are subscribed to my social media accounts. Everyone's still on the hunt, desperate to uncover the girl behind the makeup. Gabe had his cybersecurity team take down the videos from the party that spilled the beans on my identity. There are two things that sell the best in the music industry: sex and secrets. Keeping the identity of the girl behind the makeup a secret as long as possible is beneficial for all of us involved. Personally, I sort of adore the mysterious vibe and the confidence that comes with it.

Gabe and the rest of the staff at the record label want to keep the mystery going until the album drops and a tour date is released. It's a good marketing strategy, but it's hard not being able to openly talk about it. Ever since coming home after the tour a month ago, I've noticed just how much of an introvert I truly am. My place is so quiet and calm compared to being on the road with the guys.

My most exciting evening since being back home was when I hosted my parents for dinner. Now, that was an emotional evening. My mom finally came to terms with the fact I'm not returning to college. My dad finally came to terms with my success. Both of them finally realized that Aiden isn't the only one in our family who has musical talent. Once the tears and yelling were over, I played them acoustic versions of some of the songs that are going to be on the album. It ended up being a great bonding moment for the three of us. I feel as if a weight has been plucked from my chest in knowing I have their support.

"What are you thinking about?" Ashley asks.

She and I are currently on video chat and watching a movie. It's the day before the album drops, and my stomach is tied up in knots. I should be excited, but I want to hide under my blanket and become a true recluse.

"Just thinking about the album release tomorrow. And how different things are," I say as I shove a handful of popcorn into my mouth.

"It's going to be great." She claps her hands excitedly.

"I hope so." I sigh a little.

"Have you talked to Scott lately?" she asks hesitantly.

"No, we tend to stay out of each other's way." I try to keep the hurt out of my voice.

Every time Aiden comes around, Scott is always with him. This wouldn't have been a problem before, but things are different now.

"That's too bad." Ashley sighs. "He and Alissa broke up last week again for the like third time."

"Really?" I ask, a little surprised.

"I seriously don't know what he sees in her."

"I don't know," I say honestly. "She's pretty."

"You're pretty." She sighs.

Suddenly, my doorbell rings, making me jump a foot in the air.

"Somebody's here. I've got to go." I quickly end our video call.

I check my security camera and almost choke on my popcorn. Standing outside is none other than Kyle Thompson, the same Kyle I've only seen twice since we all came back to Colorado, nowhere near as often as I did while we were sharing hotels on the road. I scramble to quickly toss my hair in a ponytail and throw on a clean hoodie before opening the door.

"Kyle! What're you doing here?" I stumble in trying to get my words out. I'm equally excited and nervous at his spontaneous drop-in.

"Well, I could share with you that my schedule finally just lightened up or give you a lame excuse that I'm just in the neighborhood, but you know about the schedule already from Aiden, and it's painfully obvious I need GPS to find my way back to my apartment every time I leave it," he says with his hands shoved in his jacket pockets.

"That's pretty much all true." I chuckle. I notice Kyle shuffling his feet nervously. "What brings you to my door?" I ask curiously. My heart starts to beat a bit faster.

"I'm sort of hoping I can take you out tonight." He says it as if it's a question.

I raise an eyebrow. "Kyle Thompson, are you asking me out on a date?" I ask with genuine curiosity.

"I am." He nods firmly.

"Will there be pizza?" I lean against my door, enjoying his obvious nervousness.

"There can be." He grins.

"Great. I'll get changed real quick."

I turn and head back toward my room, leaving my door open for him to come in. I hear him come in and close the door, and my nerves jump all over the place. I'm surprised and not surprised at the same time. I could tell toward the end of the tour that something had shifted in our friendship. I would often catch him watching me when he didn't think I noticed, or he would often think of me while he was out and grab me a coffee or a snack—things that not just any friend would do.

It takes me less than fifteen minutes to throw together a cute date outfit: a pair of dark skinny jeans with a cream-colored sweater. I zip up a pair of brown boots and head out to my living room. Kyle is casually flipping through some of my music CDs and records I have sorted by the couch. He looks up when I come into the room.

"Ready to get going?" I ask, suddenly feeling nervous under his gaze.

"Sure am." He takes my hand. "You're very beautiful tonight," he says with a look that makes me blush.

I don't have a coherent answer, so I offer him a nervous smile before letting him lead me out into the evening.

We end up at a local favorite pizza spot with good drinks and music. People seem to steer clear of Kyle, or at least they don't rush up to him. I lose myself in the simplicity of the conversation and the easy way he makes me laugh. We talk about our families, his new apartment, and, of course, music. The band decides to slow things down, and a few couples head out onto the dance floor.

"May I have this dance?" Kyle holds out a hand.

"Um, I'm a terrible dancer," I say shyly.

"It's a good thing I'm not." He smiles as he pulls me out of my chair and into the mix of dancing couples.

I lean forward, resting my chin on Kyle's shoulder. He's shorter than Scott, I realize. If I tried this with Scott, my face would connect with his armpit. Then I'm annoyed with myself. I'm dancing with Kyle Thompson, who happens to be the most desirable man in the world, it seems, according to *People* magazine. Kyle is sweet to me. I like Kyle—maybe as more than a friend even. I shouldn't be thinking about Scott.

"I'm glad I came tonight," I say, wrapping my arms around Kyle's neck. "And for the record, I wish you would have called or messaged me lately. I've missed you." I sigh.

He grins. "I'm glad too. I'm sorry I didn't call. Things have been a little unorganized."

"Do you want to talk about it?" I ask as I let him sway us back and forth.

"I do but not tonight," he says sincerely.

We stay like that, two bodies swaying in the middle of a small dance floor, until the burning sun dips below the mountains, plunging the parking lot into shadows.

Two hours later, we laugh our way out into the twilight. I've missed the way Kyle can relax my nerves and make me laugh. Colorado's gray skies pull over us like an old, itchy sweater. Up ahead, Kyle motions for his driver to warm the car up. I can't help but smile at his thoughtfulness. I take a step forward, intending to make for the car, but my heel snags in a crack in the pavement. I let out a squeal, pitching forward, realizing my face is about to connect with the street. Kyle, however, catches me by scooping me completely off my feet and holding me bridal-style.

"You know," he drawls, "if you want me to hold you, you can just ask next time."

I roll my eyes playfully. "You're a narcissist, Thompson."

"Well, you're in denial."

"And you're dreaming." I breathe out.

We stare at each other, breathing hard. This close to him, I can count every eyelash on his face, smell the pepper of his cologne, and feel the warmth of his skin radiating through his shirt.

"Oh, screw it," Kyle growls, and he leans his face in to softly kiss me.

I freeze. *Oh no. No, no. I don't want this. Do I?*

Kyle slowly sets me on my feet, keeping his arms tightly around me. His hands slide down my back and up under my jacket, and I realize yes, actually, I do want this—badly.

I kiss him back with equal fervor, tangling my hands in his hair. Kyle makes a noise at the back of his throat, seemingly half surprise and half pleasure, and I can't help feeling a little smug as I press my body against his.

Kissing Scott felt like drowning, but kissing Kyle is like coming up for air. I'm able to breathe for the first time in weeks. That's when I realize I never want to stop this. So I don't. Not even when the yellow streetlights flicker on. Not even when the limo driver yawns, pausing to check his watch. Not even when the paparazzo concealed several feet away behind a large bush quietly clicks his camera.

———◆———

I know something is wrong the moment I wake up and see my phone lighting up with missed messages. My heart starts racing as I scroll through my phone. I have fifty text messages, twenty missed calls, and eight voice mails, from Ashley, Sophia, Aiden, Gabe Palman, my parents, and Julie.

I have three voice mails from Julie, which means that whatever has happened is bad.

Kyle sits up in bed with his own phone, frowning at his own notifications. "Multiple missed messages?"

"Yes." I swallow. "You don't think anyone's hurt, do you?"

I don't say what I'm actually thinking: *You don't think Scott has done something stupid, do you?*

Kyle's expression softens. "Don't worry." He reaches over to take my hand, and the gentleness is so startling that I flinch. "I'm sure Aiden's fine."

I climb out of bed and start searching for my clothes. Guilt makes my throat tight. After what happened last night, I'm pretty sure my first instinct shouldn't be to think of Scott. What the hell is wrong with me?

I punch in Ashley's number. She picks up on the first ring.

"Oh, thank God." Ashley breathes. "Did you see them yet?"

"See what?"

Ashley curses like a sailor as loudly as she can yell through the phone.

I hold my phone away from my ear until she's done. "Ash, seriously!" I yell back at her, clutching my phone tighter. "What's going on?"

"Don't go outside. Don't go online. Don't talk to anyone until this dies down," she tells me.

"What?" I ask, in shock. "I'm so confused."

"I think I know what she's talking about," Kyle tells me. "I just read a message from Aiden telling me he's working on getting me removed from the band. Followed by a link to a tabloid article featuring the two of us kissing last night." He's clearly frustrated. "I think Aiden is kidding. But I'm going to call him quick." He slides out of bed and steps out of the room to make the call.

"You're still with him?" Ashley shouts at me through the phone.

"Thanks, Ash. I'll be in touch." I end the call before she starts yelling again.

I look over at Kyle, who seems to be less agitated now that he's talking with Aiden. He even ends the call after a chuckle. He comes back in and seems to start methodically looking for the rest of his clothes.

Panic starts to set in, and I can't stop the words from tumbling out: "Please don't go." I sink into the bed and try to stop the tears from falling.

"Christ Almighty, Carly, I'm not leaving like that." Kyle bends down, scoops me up, and settles me in his lap on the bed. "Do you really think so low of me?" He runs his hands through his hair in frustration.

"No, I just …" I sniffle a few times, trying to calm down. "I didn't mean it like that," I practically blubber out.

"Yes, you did." He tilts my chin up so I can look into his eyes. "And it's OK—this time. But I need you to know that this"— he waves his phone, with all the notifications and articles on it— "doesn't bother me or dictate my choices."

I nod, not trusting myself to speak without ugly crying.

"I do need to see Aiden, though, sooner rather than later." He pinches the bridge of his nose in irritation. "I managed to calm him down from firing me outright. But he wants to have a bro-code talk." He sighs.

"I'm sorry."

"No! Don't you dare. This is not your fault or anything to apologize for. It's not your fault that your brother is a hypocrite or that the paparazzi follow me everywhere," he says with only a hint of pent-up anger.

We quickly gather our things and get ourselves sorted out. I grab us each a travel mug of coffee before we step outside into the chaos. I blink back an explosion of stars. The silvery flashes come at me like flowers bursting into life in the daylight—*pop-pop-pop*—until my vision is totally gone. Somewhere, Kyle's vision is totally gone as well, I'm sure. I hear Kyle's bodyguard shouting. I barely hear Kyle swear before pressing me protectively against his side, and it isn't until a voice shouts my name that I realize what is happening.

Paparazzi—and they aren't just here for Kyle. They are here for me too.

⟫⟨⟩⟨⟫

"You two," Julie says, seething, "are in so much trouble."

I flinch. We are gathered in the living room of Aiden's house, staring awkwardly at one another. I'm grateful Kyle delayed this meeting until after lunch. It gave me a couple of hours to check in with Gabe regarding the album sales as well as put myself together.

"I'm sorry," I say again. "If I'd known—"

"Don't." Julie holds up a hand. "Scott was one thing, Carly, but they have you on camera this time. Kissing him." She points at Kyle. "How are we supposed to deny this?"

I flinch. "Julie—"

"We don't." Kyle cuts in, casting his eyes at me. "There isn't anything to deny. I'm not a liar. I'm also not going to sit here and let you all berate Carly over this. This meeting is done. We are leaving." Kyle grabs my hand and starts pulling me across the living room.

"Wait. Hold up." Aiden finally speaks up, stopping us in our tracks. "I overreacted, and I'm sorry."

"You mean that?" Kyle raises his eyebrows. "Because your sister deserves more than that half-ass apology." He practically spits at him.

"Look, spare me the details. Just don't be an ass to her," Aiden says, looking a little green, before getting up and walking out the back door for some air.

"I, on the other hand, like the details." Cole chimes in smugly. "Particularly the kissing part." He leans back and props his feet on Aiden's coffee table. "Are you two together then?"

I feel my cheeks heat up, and I cross to the sink, deliberately keeping my eyes fixed on my large glass of cold water. "Well, we haven't—"

"Yes," Kyle says decisively. He catches my startled look. "Well, we are, aren't we?" he asks.

I clutch my water so tightly I think the glass might break. Are we? We haven't discussed it, but after last night, I can see where Kyle got the idea. And I like him. I really do. There is just one thing holding me back. As if the world can read my mind, the door comes crashing in.

"Sh! That's not being discreet." A female voice giggles. "Scott!"

"Aiden doesn't mind my having company over."

His voice is so full of fond exasperation that I feel my heart squeeze. A moment later, it plummets to my stomach as Scott comes into view, stinking of expensive alcohol and spicy cologne. Also, I realize sourly, he is sporting a bright red line of hickeys down the side of his neck. Scott freezes when he sees me.

"Carly," Scott croaks. "Why are you—" He blinks, drinking in the room. "What are you all doing here?"

"It's nice of you to bless us with your presence, Scott." Julie chastises him, causing him to flinch.

"Did I miss something?" he asks the room as a whole.

"Just a band meeting is all. Not a rehearsal this time," Cole says as he places his hands behind his head casually.

"Here." Julie sighs, flinging a magazine at him. "Have a look for yourself."

My throat dries up as Scott catches the tabloid with surprising ease, unfurling it with a snap. *Oh no. No, no, no. Shit. Should I dart forward and grab the magazine? Swat it out of his hand? Fake a heart attack?*

But it's too late.

Scott's face goes flat as he drinks in the front cover. I brace myself for the shouting. I prepare myself for cruel, cutting comments or for Scott to lose it and deck Kyle. Hell, Aiden almost did. But instead, Scott calmly rolls up the magazine; his expression is tight and controlled. Two bright red spots have appeared on his cheeks.

"What the fuck is this?" he growls.

I bite my lip. Kyle reaches over to squeeze my shoulder, and I see Scott's eyes narrow to black slits at the touch.

"It's called a kiss," Kyle says. "But I'm sure you're familiar with it." He nods at Scott's hickeys. "In fact, I know you are."

Scott's fists clench.

Beside him, Alissa sags against the doorway. "Scott," she whines, "I'm starving."

Scott ignores her. "Not now," he snaps.

"But—"

"Not now, Alissa," Scott snaps more harshly, and the girl recoils abruptly. "Christ. Can't you entertain yourself for ten bloody seconds?" He chucks the magazine at the garbage can.

Unfortunately, he is probably ten drinks deep, and his aim is sloppy; the magazine collides instead with one of Aiden's lamps, sending it shattering to the floor. I flinch.

"Scott!" Julie snaps. "Stop it."

"You're right." Scott rubs his eyes. "Sorry, Alissa. That was out of order."

I lean forward, trying to catch his eye, but he is studying the floor with apparent fascination.

"I'm tired. I'm going to bed," he says.

Alissa tilts her head. "Do you still want company?"

"No," Scott says softly. "I'll walk you out, though." He doesn't look back at me at all.

As soon as I get home, I decide it's time to call Ashley back to get things sorted out there. I groan in frustration that I still don't have things sorted out myself.

"So," Ashley says, waggling her eyebrows on the video call, "did you sleep with Kyle?"

"Ashley!" I gasp.

"Well? Did you?" Ashley prods. "Sleep with him?"

Yes, in fact, when Kyle walked me to my door and leaned in for a good-night kiss, things escalated from there to the bedroom.

"We had a nice time," I say.

Ashley smirks. "In bed?"

"Dancing," I say pointedly.

"You're no fun." Ashley pouts, taking a sip of her white wine. "Can't you kiss and tell just once? Just tell me what it was like?"

I give her a long look.

"OK, fine," Ashley says, relenting. "We'll table this conversation. For now." She takes another sip. "You said you have news?"

"Yes." I grip my drink. "My album sales are sky high!" I clap my hands as I announce the good news to her.

Ashley spews wine at the camera. "Seriously?"

"Ashley!" I say exasperatedly. "You were the one who told me it was going to be great." I point a finger at her.

"I did. I just had small doubts. But now all my doubts are gone. Thank goodness! This is fantastic!" She cheers through the phone.

"We should see the official numbers in a few days." I smile. Ashley's excitement is intoxicating.

Ashley throws her hands up. "I can't even deal! Carly, this is amazing; I'm so proud of you."

"Thanks, Ash. Can you do me a favor? Can you fill Sophia in for me?" I ask, feeling guilty about not doing it myself. "I've had a long day and just want to get some sleep."

"Sure will!" She waves goodbye before ending the call.

As soon as my head hits my pillow, I'm out like a light.

Chapter 13

I intend to speak with Scott the next morning, but instead, I oversleep. When I finally wake up and realize I have missed my alarm, panic sets in. Afternoon sunlight is already spilling into my room, drenching my cream-and-violet bedsheets in honey yellow. The clock on my bedside table informs me it's already two in the afternoon, which means I have slept for fourteen hours and missed my morning meetings.

But overall, I feel much better—rested. That is good because a missed voice mail from Julie informs me that the boys are at a radio interview downtown and that she would appreciate my bringing her a large coffee. I listen to her voice mail a couple of times, trying to comprehend what she's asking. Julie's mood swings are terrifying.

I push a few buttons and reach out to Gabe to apologize for missing the meetings. He says he understands and reschedules for tomorrow.

I stop by a coffee drive-through on my way to the radio station. I order a large cappuccino for Julie and one for myself. I briefly wonder if I should pick Kyle up something; it seems like the appropriate thing to do. I decide I owe him for countless coffees anyway and grab him a cappuccino as well.

"Oh, thank the coffee gods." Julie breathes. "I'm dying here without this."

I watch, amused, as she starts chugging the coffee with all the delicacy of a wild animal.

"I'm sorry for yesterday," Julie says finally once she has set her cup aside.

"It's OK." I shrug. "I get it."

"And also," Julie adds more determinedly, "Cole wouldn't shut up about his blind date he had, which apparently went well." She stares off into space for a moment; her cheeks turn red.

"Oh." I hesitate.

This is as close as we have ever come to discussing Julie's feelings for Cole, and I sense the situation is a lot like a water balloon: if I push too hard, it might explode, drowning us all.

I merely shrug and say, "Well, I'm here to talk if you need."

Julie gives me a grateful smile.

"How's it going?" I ask, tipping my head toward the recording booth. "Anything juicy?"

Julie snorts. "Absolutely not. I've made sure of it." She downs the rest of her coffee. "So far, they've covered hockey and the weather."

"Exciting."

"And now," Julie says, consulting her clipboard, "they're about to play a game."

"A game?"

"It's the usual stuff," Julie says, waving me off. "The radio host hooks the boys up to heart monitors and shows them pictures to see their reactions. Cute dogs. Female celebrities. Standard things."

I swallow. My palms feel sweaty, although why exactly I can't say. But I have a bad feeling about this.

In the recording studio, Cole is joking around as an assistant hooks all the boys up to the equipment.

"You're not going to electrocute us, are you?"

"Just you, Cole," Scott drawls.

"I'm just saying."

"Oy!" Aiden yells. "Look at that!" He points gleefully at the screen that displays the boys' heart rates. "I win!"

Kyle sighs. "That's not a good thing, Aiden."

"Isn't it?" Aiden asks.

"Not unless you want heart disease."

"Well, I—"

"All right, boys." The radio host interrupts, sounding exasperated. "Let's get started."

I watch, biting my lip, but Julie is right; the images are harmless. The radio host shows them drool-worthy mac and cheese, and Cole's heart rate skyrockets. Next is a clip from a horror movie with a demon, and Aiden takes that one. It isn't until the end of the interview that things go wrong.

"One last image, boys." The radio host chuckles.

The image pops up on the screen. I recognize it instantly: it's a photo taken of me last year at Sophia's birthday party in Colorado Springs. I'm leaning against the railing of a rooftop bar, with my blonde hair everywhere, laughing at something Ashley said. I can also be seen desperately attempting to pull down my silver minidress, which is halfway up my thighs.

"Well?" the radio hosts asks slyly. "Let's have it, boys."

My stomach plunges.

I exchange a look of panic with Julie, but it's too late. Scott's and Kyle's heart rates both climb, shooting up to 120. I watch with my heart in my throat as Kyle's halts at 130. Scott's heart rate, though, shoots up past 135 and still doesn't stop.

"Oh shit," Julie murmurs.

The radio host looks confused. Then, as Scott's heart rate tops 150, he looks delighted.

"Well, well," the host drawls. "That's certainly a surprise. Scott, care to explain?"

But Scott isn't looking at the host. He's looking at Aiden, who is staring up at the screen in confusion as Scott's heart rate continues to rise.

"Aiden," Scott says, "it's not what you think."

Then Aiden's expression changes. "You bastard," he growls. "That's my sister."

I watch in horror as he lunges off the chair, tackling Scott to the floor in a mess of wires.

After everyone has been separated and placed in a separate room, multiple makeup artists try to make sense of the bruises and cuts.

"Well," Julie says in a clipped voice, "I suppose we should all be thankful it wasn't a television interview. That won't be on YouTube at least."

I fiddle with a makeup brush, pushing the pad of one thumb into the bristles. Then I let them go. Push down. Let them go.

Nearby, a makeup artist is squawking over Scott's blossoming black eye, applying doses of powder.

"This is a disaster," the artist moans. "Any camera light will crucify you." He frowns, bopping Scott on the nose with the brush. "What the hell happened?"

Scott jerks his head toward the room Aiden is in. "Ask him."

Aiden has been in a stony silence since being pulled off Scott.

"Well, I think it looks very manly," Cole says loyally, munching on a handful of pretzels. "Don't you think so, Kyle?"

"I suppose." Kyle shrugs.

My throat is dry. Kyle is twirling one of his drumsticks around and around like a baton attached to a tilt-a-whirl. He hasn't spoken a single word to me since the interview earlier, and his silence is killing me. Slowly, I rise to my feet.

"Kyle," I say, "can I speak with you?"

"I think it's about time to leave," he says.

"It'll only take a moment."

"Fine." Kyle sets down the drumstick. He trails me into the corridor with the air of a reluctant soldier following his commander into battle.

"Kyle," I say, "about the interview—"

"If you like Scott," he says, interrupting me, "I wish you'd just tell me."

I swallow hard, trying to find the right words.

"Well, Scott clearly likes you," he adds.

"He doesn't, though." My words come out in a mixture of a croak and whisper.

I'm sure he doesn't. Scott made that perfectly clear when he marched into my hotel room after that night and threw it in my face and then called me his sister on national television.

"So the heart-rate-monitor thing has to be a fluke." Kyle rolls his eyes.

"He has Alissa. That was just a game," I tell him.

"Right. I'm not buying it." He shrugs.

"Look, Scott and I—" I swallow. "We have a complicated history." I cross my arms over my chest. "He's important to me. And not just because he's Ashley's brother or Aiden's best friend." I take a deep breath. "I need him. I've always needed him." I realize how lame my answer is.

"I see."

"But there's nothing going on between us," I add quickly, noting the wariness on his face. "I would tell you, Kyle."

Kyle leans against the wall, rubbing his eyes. "Look, I want to give us a shot."

"I never said—"

"But if you don't want to do this," Kyle says, ignoring me, "if you don't want to do us, then I'm not going to force you. I'll tell the press whatever you like. That the pictures are photoshopped. Or taken from a weird angle." He runs a hand through his hair. "But if you have any feelings for Scott, Carly, then I need to know. Right now."

I suck in a sharp breath. I can feel my heart hammering in my chest. This is what I've been putting off, and now that it's here, I feel sick.

I've loved Scott for years. Hell, I can hardly remember not loving Scott. But I can't deny that I feel something for Kyle too. The idea of losing him is also terrifying. He's not asking me to lie. In fact, he's asking the opposite.

"I do have feelings for Scott, Kyle. I also have feelings for you, though." I see his face looks pained. "There's something between you and me. I want to give us a shot."

"I don't think that's fair to either of us," he says after a moment. "I think it's honestly better at this point if we go the friend route." He looks as if he wants to cry.

"Kyle, I'm so sorry." I burst into tears.

Kyle, being a better person than I'll ever be, pulls me in and hugs me tightly. He holds me until my tears dry up, and I'm left exhausted and raw. Neither of us notices the pained look on Scott's face as he watches from around the corner.

⟺◆⟺

I use my album press trip to New York as a way to escape the boy drama and focus on myself and my goals. On the flight there, I rest my forehead against the plane's window as a wave of bottomless heartache and nerves courses through me. I wipe a few tears from my eyes and barely notice the airline attendant coming by with the beverage cart. The scent of freshly brewed coffee steaming on the cart hits my senses full force. I signal for a cup, and the flight attendant graciously pours one and smiles at me. I take it and sip, letting the warmth pour into the depths of my soul.

The pinging sound signaling all passengers to fasten their seat belts goes off. I quickly click my seat belt and anxiously watch as we descend back into the world below.

Since I don't have any luggage besides my carry-on, I'm able to quickly navigate the crowds of people throughout the airport to where a line of taxis and cars are waiting outside the front doors.

Wrinkling my nose at the smells of grease from stale fast food and body odor coming from the cabs, I climb into the car Gabe sent for me. I confirm the address with the driver, and he pulls out of the airport and onto the highway. The driver skillfully weaves in and out of traffic smoothly. He doesn't try to make small talk, and I'm grateful. New York brings some dreams into the reality zone. I watch the bustling city fly past the window as we drive along the streets. I can't believe I've made it out of Colorado, let alone under these circumstances.

When we arrive in front of an exquisite hotel, I realize my

dreams are truly coming true. I never will take any success from here on out for granted. I never want to stop being humble. Oddly, that's a piece of advice my brother gave me before I left for the airport.

I try to help the driver gather my carry-on for a swift entry, but he shakes his head. A little unsure, I strap my guitar to my back and then grab my purse and follow him inside. I shuffle toward the front desk while the driver hands my carry-on to a bellhop. Once I give the front desk lady my name, she promptly hands me a key card and instructions for the free internet. I thank her sincerely and make my way to the elevator.

"It looks like you're on one of the top floors; you're going to love the beautiful view." The bellhop presses a few buttons on the elevator keypad and then scans a hotel key card.

The doors open, and we get inside for the lift.

I follow the bellhop down a couple of halls before arriving in front of my hotel door. I quickly slide my key card through, and a stunning, spacious room greets me. There's a small wall as I walk in, with a grand mirror, which acts as a barrier for privacy. I walk to the left and see the beautifully styled living room and the open kitchen to the right.

Stunning full-length floor-to-ceiling windows open the room up to an enchanting view of the city buildings. Behind me is another door, which I find leads to a bedroom with the same stunning view. I could easily get used to this lifestyle. I take my carry-on suitcase from the bellhop and hand him a tip.

"Don't hesitate to call guest services if you require anything during your stay," he says with a smile before exiting and closing the door behind him.

I off-load my belongings and continue to explore the room. As

I'm searching through stuff, my phone rings, startling me. I'm even more startled to see that Julie is calling me.

"Julie? What's up?" I answer, propping my phone between my cheek and my shoulder.

"Carly, I have a serious question. Do you have a manager yet?" she asks in her business tone.

This is an unexpected conversation.

"Um, well, no, not exactly," I say, unsure. "I haven't been able to click with any of the prospects. I've been sort of winging it and thanking the Lord that Gabe and his team aren't treating me like an idiot."

"Would you like me to step in?" she asks, still businesslike but friendlier. "I honestly don't mind. I swear I'll keep it all separate from Shade," she says earnestly.

"Honestly, I would love that, Julie." I smile as I look out the window at the view. "I'm sorry I didn't think to talk to you about this sooner."

"Don't stress about it. It's been a crazy few months," she says, sounding relieved.

"Well, I have some press things here in New York. Is it wrong of me to want you here now?" I ask, hoping she can make it happen.

"I was hoping you would say that," she says with a laugh. "Aiden told me you left for New York this morning, so I flew out here on a whim, hoping you would want me to join you." She sounds nervous again.

"Seriously? You are the best! Yes! The hotel room I'm in has three bedrooms. I don't know why, but it does. So just come stay with me!" I clap my hands excitedly.

"Fantastic. Text me your location, and I'll be there within the hour. I just landed," she says.

"You got it!"

"Oh, and, Carly? Please don't forget to eat lunch before any interviews. I know you're nervous, but seriously, eat something," she says, sounding businesslike again.

"Fine," I groan. "See you soon." I smile as I hang up the call.

I quickly call down to the front desk to give the receptionist Julie's information and say she'll be staying with me. My request is immediately granted without hesitation and met with wonderful customer service. I thank the person on the line and send a quick message to Julie, letting her know she's all set at the front desk.

I can't help but think how well things are falling in line. It's as if the cosmic universe is finally on my side. I text Julie the hotel address and room number before walking into the kitchen in search of a food menu. There's a small leather binder with the word *Menu* stylistically written across the front in fancy golden letters. I flick through the pages to find the lunch section.

The first thing my eyes land on is a beautifully crafted grilled cheese. My mouth instantly waters at the prospect of a good, crispy grilled cheese sandwich. The menu instructs guests to press the number-two button to go to room service. I find the wireless phone on the table and order the food I want before progressing back to the bedroom to organize what I've brought to wear.

A half hour quickly passes without my realizing it. There's a knock on the door, which sends butterflies erupting in my stomach. I'm not entirely ready to face the world just yet, especially with one eye of makeup. I look ridiculous.

I suck in some courage as I walk toward the door. I open it

to find a young man no older than I am staring back at me. The man's cobalt-blue eyes scan over my body, which makes me shiver. I suddenly wish I had either Scott or Kyle here with me. Seeing this attractive man gives me lonely vibes.

"Delivery of grilled cheese and fruit," he says, trying to hold off the smile itching to spread across his lips.

"Yes," I whisper, avoiding his intense gaze.

He removes a silver tray from the cart behind him and hands it to me. The tray is surprisingly warm and light in my hands.

"Thank you," I say.

"Have a nice day." He smiles.

I smile in return and then watch as he walks down the hall and disappears around another corner. I heave a sigh of relief as I close the door. I backtrack to the lounge room and plop onto the plush couch. I take the lid off the tray, and a puff of steam floats up and stings my face, but the sweet aroma of grilled cheese makes my stomach growl.

I find the television remote on the coffee table in front of me. Without someone telling me what to watch, I flick to the cartoon channel and settle back into the chair. I start chomping through the first triangle of the sandwich as a silly rerun of an old cartoon plays on the screen. Like anyone else, I get sucked into the motion of watching television.

After I finish eating, I place the tray on the table and sprawl out on the couch, hugging a soft cushion to my chest. My calm is only disturbed by the sound of another person entering the hotel room.

"Carly? Are you getting ready?" Julie calls out.

The familiar sense of guilt trickles into my stomach and makes me feel sick. I'm not even close to being ready! I can't believe I let a cartoon suck me into not being able to complete my only task.

I push my body up and rest my chin on the back of the couch as I look for the physical appearance of Julie. She walks along the wall and stands a few feet away from me. She seems distracted by something on her phone, and I use that to my advantage to slip away.

"Working on it," I call out midway through my escape to the bedroom.

"Seriously?" she asks with a chuckle.

"I'm sorry," I tell her as she enters my room.

I pick up the eyeliner pencil and finish where I left off. I dab and goop up my eyes with accentuating makeup and then gather the rest of my belongings for my handbag. Before leaving the room, I check over my outfit and straighten out any wrinkles.

My blue jeans are tight-fitting but show off the curves of my hips, while my fitted white top, which flares out around my hips, accentuates my hourglass figure. When I'm happy with my completion, I find my black flats sitting at the end of the bed.

"Are you ready yet?" Julie asks once more.

"I was born ready!" I tease. I walk over and give her a genuine hug. "I really appreciate you coming here and wanting to help me with all of this."

"Well, we are practically family at this point." She chuckles. "And family sticks together. Also, before I forget to let you know, I've booked a nice table for dinner tonight," she says without looking up from her phone.

"Sounds fun." I smile. The idea of a nice time out is intriguing. It's been a while since I've had a calm, nice dinner out.

"Let's get moving."

I follow Julie's lead out of the hotel room and toward the elevator.

We slip through the lobby and out the front to find the waiting car. A swirl of good nerves float through my stomach, but the same chilling, worried feeling is there. Standing in New York reminds me I've been thrown into a whole new world, and I've yet to find my feet. Will I hit the ground running or fall on my face?

Chapter 14

W hen I hear the word *paparazzi,* my first thoughts are of blaring voices, blinding lights, and people running to get away—in short, chaos. When I think back to the time before my album release a month ago, I miss what my normal was and no longer is. Ever since the record label finally released my identity as the girl behind the makeup in a simple music video we put together, life has been a whole lot more complicated.

I've been followed by random strangers for miles and asked for countless autographs and fan photos, and I even had to move into a house of my own with around-the-clock security. I have my parents and Aiden to thank for helping me get all of that taken care of back in Colorado. There's zero chance I would have been able to take care of it on my own on top of flying to Los Angeles and New York for press events. The back-and-forth time zone changes are starting to wear on me.

Kyle and Cole send me off-and-on reminders to find the bright side of things and to enjoy it—all of it, including the long-lensed cameras and crazy fans. I have a few more days of press and photographs in Los Angeles, and then I'll be heading back home to Colorado.

"You know, I like the cover of *Cosmo* better," Ashley says. "It has a cute shot of you leaning on a bridge. But the *Sun* is good too. They've touched up your skin to make it look shiny."

I roll my eyes. With the way the sun has been beating down these days, I'm sure my skin is shiny right now too but not in a good way. I adjust my sweaty baseball cap. God, what I would give to take it off. But I can't risk it, not here in a public restaurant with so many cameras around.

"Hey." I frown. "My skin is not really that bad."

"It's dry."

"I'm from Colorado," I say defensively.

"I'm just saying."

I pause to look around the dining area of the restaurant to see if anyone is paying attention. Thankfully, nobody is. The smells of fancy wine, steaks, and seafood fill the air. Ashley flew into town a few days ago for some serious girl time. For that, I'm grateful. Julie is great, but a girl needs her best friend sometimes.

"I'm thinking of throwing a small concert back home when I get back," I say, nibbling my lip. "You don't think that's stupid, do you?"

"It's perfect." Ashley claps her hands. "Everyone back home is so excited for you."

"I need to get Julie on it. Work out the details and such."

"You haven't talked to her about it yet?" Ashley makes a noise somewhere between a shriek and the braying of a horse.

"No." I frown slightly. "But I think I will later today. I think I'm going to do it."

"We're throwing a party," Ashley says decisively. "As soon as we get back to Colorado." She sighs happily. "I love parties."

"They don't love you," I say, thinking of the times in the past when I've had to hold back Ashley's hair as she vomited in the early hours of the morning.

"It'll be a launch party for just everyone back home, Carly," Ashley says, sounding exasperated.

"I'm not sure anyone besides you, Sophia, and Cole would even really want to come," I mutter.

"More people than you think. Everyone is so proud of you, Carlz."

"I suppose."

"Well, Cole will come," Ashley says firmly. "And so will Kyle. And Scott." She hesitates. "I mean, if you want him there."

I pause, taking a drink of my wine. There is a long, awkward silence. I swallow, gripping my glass before setting it down out of fear of snapping it. This is the closest we've come to discussing what happened that day at the radio station. I know Ashley must have listened to the interview—hell, practically the whole world has—but she has never brought it up with me. Until now.

"Scott can come," I say, turning my attention to my chicken salad. "Why wouldn't he be invited?"

"Carly." Ashley hesitates. "You know that Scott—"

"He's with Alissa."

"But the radio thing. I really think—"

"There was clearly a misunderstanding somewhere," I say, cutting her off. "He's made his decision loud and clear."

"What are you talking about?" she asks, surprised.

Well, shit. Might as well come clean now, I think.

"Scott and I slept together." I watch many reactions cross over her face. "And afterward, he told me it was a mistake and that I'm basically his sister, which he said again on national television."

The profanities that come out of Ashley's mouth are so bad that I ask for the check, pay for our meals, and pull her out of the restaurant. She's ready to tear her brother's throat out by the time we get back to the hotel. Knowing Ashley, she would hop a plane tonight and have Scott murdered and the body buried by morning at this rate. That makes me nervous to leave her to her own devices.

I decide to call Julie for reinforcements, which proves to be zero help. As soon as Ashley spills the beans on the situation to Julie, Julie is equally ready to murder Scott. I'm both flattered and frustrated by their outbursts.

"Will you both cut it out?" I yell over the incessant shouting.

They both clamp their mouths shut.

"This is all a moot point. Scott made his position loud and clear, so he and I never went further than the bedroom. Kyle called me out, and I was honest; that's why he and I aren't together. So please just stop." I collapse into a chair, emotionally exhausted. It's unfair that Scott seems to be getting off free, while I can't seem to move past it all.

"You're right, Carly. Yelling and getting mad isn't going to change anything," Julie says as she kneels in front of me, and I watch her exchange a look with Ashley. "But I might have an idea on what will."

"Am I going to like this idea?" I ask as I rub my temples to ease the headache that's approaching.

"It depends." Julie shrugs.

"On what?"

"On how much you trust us."

"I'm still lost."

"You know, Carly, it might be better if Julie and I work out these details while you get some sleep." Ashley kneels in front of me as well and gives me a hug.

"I'm too tired right now to even try to argue." I let out a sigh into her shoulder.

"I know." She rubs my back. "Go get some sleep."

⟫◈⟪

The final bit of press finally wraps up over the next forty-eight hours, and I'm drained, physically and emotionally. Between hair and makeup for this and that, I start to wonder if all the hairspray will come out. Julie and Ashley have packed all my bags for me since we are leaving for the airport as soon as my last radio interview wraps up.

I give a laugh or two at a few jokes and answer some fan questions. The radio host tries to prod for a tour date, but I eloquently evade the question with a general answer: "We haven't set anything in stone yet. Gabe is hoping to have the schematics worked out by the end of the year."

Thankfully, the host picks up on it and decides not to push. We wrap the interview, and I'm ushered from the station straight to the waiting car.

I relish the quiet of the plane ride, opting for some extra sleep. I still don't know what Julie and Ashley are up to, and I'm not sure I want to know. Julie has the concert all squared away at one of the local joints, and it's quickly become a hot ticket. I decide not to question how she's managed to pull it off. She reminds me that it's technically the first concert I'll perform, since a tour hasn't been officially announced, which sends my anxiety and nerves to new heights.

⟫◈⟪

I'm slowly becoming undone by nerves. The bar is packed, with a line spilling into the parking lot. The local joint Julie has booked can barely fit the crowds who have turned up. Ashley confirms with a bartender that it's basically standing room at this point. I swallow the lump in my throat for the zillionth time, lifting my sticky blonde hair off my damp neck. I adjust my guitar on my lap and start tuning it.

God, I wish Scott would come. He used to be the only one who could calm me down before choir concerts and school performances. *What has he always said?* "*The only person you need to impress is yourself.*" *Easier said than done.*

A hand lands on my shoulder, startling me out of my thoughts. I jump about five feet in the air with a squeal, whipping around, and the culprit in question raises her arms.

"Easy!" Sophia says. "It's just me."

"You scared me!" I work to calm my racing heart.

"Obviously." Ashley thrusts out an arm. "Here. This soda water should help."

I uncap the bottle and take a sip. I swish the liquid around before swallowing and then take a larger sip. It's not a perfect remedy, but it'll help me to keep my last meal down.

Ashley and Sophia look at me with genuine concern. We've spent the last two hours in my dressing room, watching a trashy reality show and eating popcorn. Well, Ashley has been eating popcorn; I've been too nervous to do much of anything, hence the soda water. Fortunately, I'm saved from any further anxious thoughts by the appearance of a frazzled Gabe Palman, who has a cigarette tucked behind his ear and a walkie-talkie earpiece in his other. I realize my anxiety hasn't really gone down. Gabe is rarely frazzled and never in public.

"You're all set?" he asks.

"I'm all set." I nod.

"You remember your lyrics?" he asks gruffly.

"I hope so," I say, feeling a bit green all of a sudden.

"You won't trip?" He motions to my heels I have yet to put on.

"If this is your way of wishing me luck," I mutter, "you're doing a terrible job." I pick at the sleeve of my brown leather jacket.

"All right, I get it. I'll leave you alone. Showtime in fifteen minutes," Gabe says before he disappears once more.

"You need to distract me." I turn to Sophia and Ashley.

"What?" Sophia says.

"I'm spiraling." I grip Sophia's shoulders. "Tell me something good."

"Oh. Um." Sophia blinks, seemingly caught off guard. "Scott and Alissa broke up a while ago for good."

I stare at her. *Out of everything she can say, she chooses that?*

"I hate you," I mutter, letting go of her shoulders. "You have terrible timing."

"Well, I might know a way to cheer you up," Ashley says with a smile as she looks behind me toward the doorway.

"Have I mentioned that I'm going to pass out?" I groan, on the verge of a panic attack.

"If you do," a voice says, "I'll be sure to catch you."

I whip around so fast that it takes me a few minutes to register and comprehend what I'm seeing. Scott stands half concealed in the shadows of the hallway. His hands are stuffed in his pockets; his dark hair is a mess. His white V-neck shirt is a crisp contrast to the black tattoo on his forearm, which is uncovered by his rolled-up sleeves. My stupid heart lurches into my throat. He looks like a hot mess but somehow still ruggedly handsome and completely Scott. And he is here. He is actually here.

"Hi, Carlz," he says softly.

"Would you mind …" I trail off as I turn to Sophia and Ashley.

"Oh, I definitely have somewhere more important to be." Sophia rolls her eyes playfully.

They step out of the dressing and close the door behind them, leaving the two of us alone.

I listen to their footsteps retreating. I can't tear my eyes away from Scott. His green eyes gleam in the dim lighting, the color of sunshine through spring leaves.

"You broke up with Alissa?" I ask after a moment.

"Yes, a while ago."

"How come?" I can't help but ask. "Honestly, I thought the two of you were going strong."

Scott takes a step closer. He smells of rustic forest and fresh rain. He lifts a hand to my face, and my eyes flutter closed. A warm thumb strokes my jaw.

"I'm sorry," he murmurs. "For everything. I've been an absolute ass. That night of the party, I thought—" His warm breath tickles my neck. "I didn't think you wanted more."

My eyes fly open. "Seriously?"

"I didn't exactly give you room to set me straight. I'm a complete ass."

"You said that already." My lips twitch slightly into a grin.

"It needs to be repeated," Scott says solemnly. "Possibly several more times."

"You didn't speak to me." My heart hammers. "For weeks after, I thought you hated me. You called me your sister. On television."

"Not my finest moment." Scott winces.

"Not at all."

He shuffles his feet. "I was going to speak with you about it, but then you and Kyle—" His hand tightens on my chin. "It killed me to watch that, Carly. Killed me. But I thought"—his throat bobs—"if you were happy, then I would stay silent."

"You got back together with Alissa so fast I truly thought I didn't matter." My breath catches in my throat.

"Another not-so-fine moment of mine. Aiden had asked me to bring a date to some publicity ordeal, and Alissa was available. Between the tabloids and all the other bullshit ..." He trails off. "Well, let's just say both Alissa and I let that go too far."

Heat sweeps through my body. I think back to the day many years ago when I first saw Scott shirtless and felt as if an invisible hundred-pound weight landed in my stomach.

Oh, I thought, *so this is what it feels like to love someone.*

That feeling grew over the years, twisting and maturing into something else, but it is still lodged in my heart—that little bubble of excitement, that tiny piece of Scott.

"What are you saying?" I whisper.

Scott swallows. "I'm trying to say that I—"

"Taylor!"

We both turn. A visibly irritated bald man in a headset is gesturing frantically at me, and it takes me a moment to come back into my body and realize the crowd is buzzing with excitement. Somewhere, a bass begins to thump.

"Shit." My nerves return in a flood. "That's my cue."

"Are you OK?"

"No." I pause. "But I'm going out there anyway."

Scott winks. "That's my girl." He drops his hand. "I'll be watching from the crowd. Come find me after."

I shift my guitar, bracing myself. Then I step out onto the stage. It's brighter than I remember—much brighter. In fact, I suspect I won't have retinas at the end of the night. I step up to the microphone and strum the first few chords on my guitar.

The buzzing of the crowd intensifies, and cameras start flashing everywhere.

I swallow the lump of nerves in my throat hard again.

There are wishes you make when you blow out the candles on a birthday cake, and there are wishes you tell only your closest friends. Then there is the one all-consuming wish that petrifies you, the wish you can't even admit aloud, the secret dream knitted into your heart.

This is it. This is my wish.

I take a deep breath.

"Everybody ready for a good time?" I shout into the microphone.

The crowd cheers.

I can't help but grin. Miraculously, my anxiety is seeping away, replaced with a sense of relief.

I've got this.

I begin to play. The house band's drummer picks up the beat and follows my lead, and a low hum falls over the crowd. Then the amp kicks in, with the bass guitar following shortly. The crowd cheers.

Then I begin to sing, and the crowd sings with me.

> I know you tell the world lies,
> but all I need is for you to try.
> I can't sit, can't stand, can't wait.

You always take these girls' bait.
I play your voice in the background.
Just to turn my frown
upside down.
But lately, just lookin' in your eyes
causes nothin' but late-night cries.

My heart expands until I think it might burst. They are singing my lyrics. They know my song.

We're standing on a mountain peak.
You won't take the leap.
I know I've gotta let you go.
It breaks my soul.
Distance hasn't given clarity.
I might need some back-road therapy.

I play a second song. And a third one. And a fourth one.

I play until my entire set list is finished. I strum the final chords to the last song while everyone in the place applauds. The clapping echoes like fireworks in the room. I can't stop grinning. Nothing could make this better. Nothing except—

My heart stops.

The spotlight pauses on one high-top table off to the side of the crowd. Sophia and Ashley are jumping up and down at the table like mad. Julie, Kyle, and Cole are whistling and applauding. My parents are there too, smiling. Beside them, I realize with my heart in my throat, Aiden is on his feet, whistling and grinning at me.

And Scott is there too.

I catch his gaze. Scott looks up at me with so much fierce pride on his face that it is almost painful to look at him. His cheeks are flushed red. My throat feels thick. I'm vaguely aware of the irritable tech guy waving at me.

"Get off," he hisses. "Off the stage!"

I do exactly that. But I don't exit through the side door the tech guy is gesturing to. Instead, I sprint for the stairs leading down to the main floor.

"Not that way!" the tech guy shouts after me.

But I'm not listening. The spotlight chases me as I race through the crowd. I'm vaguely aware of everyone trying to get my attention for a photo or a handshake, but it all feels far away, distant. The only thing that seems real to me is Scott.

He looks stunned. "Carly?" he says. "What are you—"

But I don't answer. Instead, I lunge at him and kiss him squarely on the mouth.

The audience bursts into hysterics. Scott goes stiff with surprise, but his arms come up automatically around me. I wrap my legs around his waist, pulling him closer. Then he kisses me back. It's the best feeling in the world, I decide dizzily. Better than espresso running through my veins. Better than the adrenaline rush that comes with performing. I feel as if someone has just stabbed an electric rod directly into my heart. When I finally come up for air, Scott's eyes are clouded.

"What was that? Did we—"

"Yeah," I whisper, kissing him on the nose.

"Did you just kiss me?"

"I did."

"In front of everyone?"

"Yes."

"In front of your parents?"

"Correct."

"You're mad," Scott says, shaking his head. "Talk about ripping the Band-Aid off." He grins. "I love you, Carly Taylor."

I cup his cheeks in my hands and look him squarely in the eyes. "I love you too, Scott."

I slide down him, ignoring the *click-click* of cameras as I take his hand. "Want to get out of here?"

"With you?" Scott squeezes my hand. "I'll go anywhere."

Printed in the USA
CPSIA information can be obtained
at www.ICGtesting.com
LVHW040548261123
764762LV00053B/1505